What does not destroy me makes me strong.

For my Mum, Dad and Chloe, thanks for all of the support.

Special thanks to my proof readers: Aaron Roberts, Ian Cummings and to all the guys on Webook, Wattpad and Authonomy, that have given advice and inspired me to keep going throughout the process.

Finally a special mention to the winning Facebook fans:

Joel Stinton,

Deea Sterea ,

Scott Bishop,

Benjamin J Snider

and Robert K. Blechman

Blood of kings

Unconquered: Book One

By
Matthew Olney

Characters

Acca *Saxon warrior and sworn man of Osfrid*

Aerlene *Wife of Osfrid*

Ceadda *Captain and squire of Driffield*

Cearl of **Acomb** *A Thegn of Northumberland*

Ealdred *Archbishop of York*

Edward the Confessor *King of England*

Edwin *Earl of Mercia*

Esma *Osfrid's daughter*

Gyrth Godwinson: *Earl of East Anglia,*

Gulbrandr: *Mercenary*

Handel: *Tostig's man*

Harold Godwinson: *Lord of Wessex*

Harald Hardrada: *King of Norway*

Hunweld:	*Osfrid's father*
Leofwine	*Earl of Kent*
Morcar	*Earl of Northumbria*
Osfrid Hunweldsen	*Thegn of Driffield*
Olaf fork-beard	*Slave master*
Ragner Oakenson	*Viking*
Tostig Godwinson	*Exiled earl*
Velmud	*Varangian*
William the bastard	*Duke of Normandy*
Wulf	*Son of Osfrid*
Waltheof	*Earl of East Anglia*

Part One

The coming Storm

1.

October 1065

York

Flames leapt up from the thatched roofs, blinding the panic stricken populace; their screams of terror breaking the early morning birdsong.

An angry crowd stormed through the mud and filth of the now devastated town, eager to exact their revenge upon their lord's hall.

The Thegns barracks were the first to be put to the flame and, like a spark it ignited the frenzy of violence that followed.

The people had finally grown tired of their lord, whose rule had cost them dearly in taxes and injustices.

Upon seeing the mob advancing towards them, the few guards stationed outside of Earl Tostig's mote and bailey castle dropped their spears and ran away into the town's smoke filled streets. A cheer rose from the mob as they saw the defenders flee; a renewed determination coursed through their ranks.

Just as the crowd reached the castle's heavy gates, a horn sounded over the clamour of violence, and looting. The crowd slowed, watching as the large oak gates swung open.

There, before them, was a warrior astride a black stallion. His magnificent armour reflected the sunlight, giving him an unearthly appearance. He wore a silver helmet, and a faceplate that covered his features, of which, only the cold hard eyes could be seen.

The crowd slowed and eventually stopped, not wanting to incur the wrath of the horseman; on his back was a large round wooden shield and buckled to his belt was a scabbard holding a golden hilted sword. Those at the front were jostled and shoved, as other rioters joined the back of the crowd, desperate to get to the castle and the promise of loot within. Some made the sign of the cross as they saw the warrior.

"Any man, who tries to pass me, dies!" bellowed the warrior.

With that, the crowd fell silent. None of them wanted to die at his hands. An eerie silence descended the sounds of battle and looting could still be heard in the distance as other parts of the town succumbed to the attackers.

The sound of galloping hooves caused the mob to move aside as a group of five warriors rode through their ranks; they pulled to a stop outside the castle. The leader glared at the defiant lone warrior. His companions dismounted and warily approached the gate.

"I am Thegn Cearl of Acomb. Under decree of the king, you are to step aside, and surrender the traitor Tostig Godwinson to us on pain of death."

The lone warrior stared out at the Thegn and his men. Each wore chainmail and carried a shield emblazoned with the Saxon dragon; they all carried a spear and sword. The black stallion flared its nostrils and whinnied breaking the tension that had descended upon them.

"You cannot pass." The warrior stated simply as he loosened his sword in its scabbard.

Cearl scowled, impatient and annoyed that some fool would stand in his way. He rubbed his temple wearily.

"What is your name?" He demanded, as he nodded to his men, they readied their spears and began to advance cautiously onto the lone warrior.

Each of them was a Housecarl, skilled and deadly warriors and every one of them had probably stood in the shield wall during battle.

"My name is Osfrid Hunweldsen, Thegn of Driffield, sworn man of Tostig Godwinson. And I say you have no right to take him. You are not doing the Kings bidding, but that of Morcar" The horseman replied.

"Then Osfrid Hunweldsen, you will die, you insolent bastard."Cearl snapped.

Osfrid narrowed his eyes as he watched the slow approach of his adversaries. He cast a quick glimpse behind him and was relieved to see his wife and children leave the castle's main hall, slipping out of the secret passage he had shown them earlier that morning, as of his lord Tostig, there was no sign. He assumed the wretch would make a stand in his hall rather than meekly surrender to his nemesis.

Thegn Morcar had summoned the Thegns of the North to depose Tostig, claiming he had become a tyrant to the people.

Osfrid agreed with that description, but it wasn't Morcar's right to declare war upon him. Such an action threatened the possibility of civil war, something that the kingdom could ill afford whilst its enemies circled like vultures, just waiting to snatch the crown from the childless Edwards head.

No doubt the rest of his personal guard would be waiting with him, unlike the other guards who dropped their weapons and joined the looting mobs as they sacked York. He smiled to himself; he'd fulfilled his duty to his family. They were now safe, there was no point in him dying to save Tostig, and the man was a wretch.

He turned back to face Thegn Cearl and his men and was about to stand down and let them pass, when suddenly one of the warriors charged.

As the warrior hurled his spear, Osfrid swore under his breath as he tried to lead his horse out of the way, but the spear struck his mount, piercing hide and flesh.

Blood sprayed and the horse whinnied, bucking violently, throwing Osfrid onto the soft muddy ground with a heavy thud.

Quickly he rolled to his left, as his eager attacker chopped down with his sword, narrowly missing his head. He could see his attacker was young, no more than seventeen, no doubt eager to prove him-self in battle.

The slaying of a well armoured warrior would earn the boy great renown amongst his peers. It was that eagerness that gave the young warrior his speed, but it also made him clumsy.

Osfrid parried a quick series of thrusts with his own drawn sword. The crowd began to cheer viciously as they sensed blood was about to be spilt, no doubt bets were being made amongst them.

He hesitated, throwing a quick glance behind him. His trusty steed collapsed to the ground, its blood spilling onto the dirt. With a last snort for air the horse lay still.

He parried again, and this time stepped close slamming the heavy hilt of his sword into the young warrior's stomach, winding him in the process. The warrior staggered back desperately gasping for air; he managed two gulps before Osfrid swung his blade in a mighty arc and cut deep into the boy's neck, only his mail coif preventing the blade from taking his head off completely. Blood sprayed everywhere, covering the now grimacing Thegn Cearl.

Once again silence fell on the crowd. They were stunned as they watched the young man's almost headless torso fall to its knees before crumpling into the mud.

"My lord, enough of this!" Osfrid shouted as he wiped his blood covered blade on his sleeve and stood to face the other now, nervous warriors. He lowered his sword and walked towards Cearl.

"I wish no further bloodshed; I surrender my blade to you." Osfrid shouted, as he plunged his sword into the muddy ground. He then stepped away and raised his arms in surrender.

Cearl dismounted and stepped forward taking the hilt of Osfrid's sword and pulled it out of the ground. He held it up and studied the hilt which had the golden figure of a dragon emblazoned upon it.

With that he gestured to his surviving men to restrain Osfrid.

"I remember you Osfrid, and I remember this sword, your fathers I believe?' He said raising an eyebrow. 'I also served with your uncle in Wales. I would have thought you would have found a more worthy Lord to follow than Tostig" The Thegn said as he raised the faceplate on the restrained fighter's helmet.

A set of hard blue eyes looked out at him, the man had a disjointed nose that had been broken years before, and his face was covered by a sharply trimmed blond beard. A colour that the hair on his head shared as wisps could be seen dangling onto his forehead.

Sadness was evident on Cearl's face as he looked at the blood soaked corpse lying in the mud. The Thegn looked away from the body and then at Osfrid.

"I had often thought that his reckless ambition to prove himself a great warrior would end badly', the Thegn sighed and shrugged his shoulders as he gazed down. "He was my nephew,' He said sadly, "His mother will be distraught."

*

The heavy oak doors splintered and buckled inwards sending splinters flying into the hall. The high pitched squeal of breaking timbers and shattering hinges resonated through the castles main chamber. The large earthen fireplace that dominated the back of the place had been quenched moments before to lessen the threat of the wooden building being consumed by fire. All of the wooden furniture, including the massive dining table had been pushed against the now breached entryway as a barrier.

Tostig Godwinson drew his sword and bellowed for his men to take up positions on either side of the entryway. Standing in his chainmail armour and wearing his heavy green cloak he looked the very vision of a warrior. His green eyes stared at the doorway that threatened to give way. Idly, he stroked his ginger tinged beard as he studied the faces of his faithful men. Some showed fear, but most only wore the calm expression of a man who was about to face death.

He assumed that Osfrid was dead; at least he hoped he was. He had known for many months that the Thegn of Driffield had only pledged his loyalty because of the threat Tostig posed to his family's lands. In some ways he admired Osfrid's ability to lie so cunningly, it reminded him of himself. A talent for survival was an invaluable trait in these turbulent times.

They called him a tyrant, a title that he secretly relished, so what if he taxed the poor or executed those who spoke out against him, the king would need someone like him to save the kingdom from Tostig's bastard of a brother Harold.

The two Godwinson brothers had fought for the king in Wales a decade previously and upon their return they had been hailed as heroes by the people. Now, Tostig found himself about to fight the followers of a fellow Thane.

He was shaken out of his thoughts by the crash of the hall doors bursting open. For a moment there was a pause. A tense silence filled the hall as Tostig's men readied themselves to fight; he himself kissed the hilt of his sword and whispered a silent prayer.

A flaming torch flew through the breached doorway, and landed against one of the walls. Tostig yelled for someone to extinguish the flame but was interrupted, as with a howl his enemies stormed through the entryway.

At once the place was filled with the deafening sounds of battle, screams and cries echoed all around. Tostig watched as his men viciously cut down the first wave of attackers, but to his dismay they were instantly replaced by more. The naked flame now caught on a banner that decorated one of the walls. The cloth quickly set ablaze darkening the wood underneath until it too began to burn. Smoke began to swirl around the struggling figures making visibility difficult.

A spear thrust narrowly missed his head, causing him to duck and lash out with his own weapon. He smiled as he felt the satisfying sensation of his blade sinking deeply into another man's flesh. He wrestled his blade free from the body, slashing at any figures in his way, friend or foe.

The smoke stung his eyes making it difficult to breathe; he could just make out the shape of the doorway and the outside through the swirling smoke, it promised sweet fresh air. Within moments the fire had burst into an inferno as the thatched roof caught ablaze, debris began to collapse into the hall striking warriors or engulfing the wounded and dying.

Desperately he fought his way to the entryway. With a swing of his sword he dispatched two warriors taking them both in the throat. He could feel blood soak his face, but he didn't stop, he glanced about him and could see the fighting had ended, as all of the combatants; both friend and foe alike now fled the deadly fire. He clawed his way through them, pushing and jostling, until finally the feeling of intense heat faded and was replaced by the cold October air.

He collapsed to his knees, coughing and retching uncontrollably and saw that all around him others were doing the same. Some laughed as they realised that they had made it out alive. Others just collapsed from their wounds, or moaned in pain from burns, or other injuries.

"There he is!" came a shout.

"Kill the bastard!" yelled another.

He looked up and saw a large crowd of peasants approaching; at their head was a horseman wearing the armour of a noble. For a moment he contemplated running but he knew he was in no condition to do so. Staggering onto his feet, he waited for the crowd's approach.

"Tostig Godwinson, do you surrender?" called the rider as his men rounded up Tostig's followers and began confiscating weapons and binding their hands.

Tostig spat onto the ground at the horseman's feet and glared up at him contemptuously.

"So Cearl, how long have you been Morcar's lapdog?' He said defiantly; "Only the King has the power to depose me of my lands, not scum like you."

Thegn Cearl narrowed his eyes, "Arrogant until the end." He sneered; "Morcar may be the one, who leads us, but the king will back us in this, the land has no need for tyrants like you."

"You had better pray that my brother takes your side Cearl, you know what Harold is capable of when his family is threatened." Tostig mocked.

He knew his brother would not back the rebellious nobles; they had been through too much together. With the power that Harold wielded being the Kings right-hand man, he would hang Morcar and the others.

Confident that his brother would see him freed Tostig laughed. A laugh that was taken up by his now bound and stripped men. The laugh echoed through the autumn air, as the town of York was engulfed in flames.

***

2.

The smoke from York could be seen from miles around. The grey autumn sky mingled with the rising ash, creating black clouds that caused the sky to turn a darker shade of grey.

Down at a nearby stream, huddled together, was Osfrid's wife and two children. Wrapped tightly about her was a red woollen cloak that she draped over her son and daughter to keep them warm. Her cotton dress was covered in mud and filth from the fields and streets they had to cross to reach the copse of trees that Osfrid had instructed them to go to.

Aerlene was full of worry for her husband. He had always said that Tostig's actions would bring the wrath of the other nobles down upon his head. The man had once been hailed a champion for the people, but somewhere along the road he had lost his way, as Osfrid always said 'power corrupts'.

She brushed back a strand of long auburn hair from her face and glanced around at the clearing. All around them were trees, now bare thanks to the coming of autumn. Osfrid had said that he would meet them here if he too could escape.

"Where is papa?" asked her son quietly. The lad was only ten years old and already he was beginning to look like his father. His head of blond hair and clear blue eyes sent a pang of sorrow through Aerlene. His name was Wulf, after her father, a fitting name for the lad, as he was often running about the place like his namesake.

"He's helping Thegn Tostig son." Replied Aerlene calmly. She didn't want to panic the boy any further than he already was. All throughout his young life he had relied on his father to protect him -- they all had.

"Why does he help that turd Mama? The man is the Devil's spawn." The eldest of the children said.

Esma was her name, and at the age of fourteen she was considered an adult. Osfrid had been looking for a suitable husband for her to marry and had been through many potential suitors for his daughter. None of them ever matched up to his expectations however, and the young woman remained a maiden.

"Don't speak like that in front of your brother Esma" Aerlene said angrily "Your father has no choice but to work for him. If he didn't then Tostig would have driven us out of our home long ago."

Since the year before, their lands had been in danger of Tostig's fearsome temper. Two Thegns had come to Tostig to complain against his harsh treatment of the people. Gamel and Ulf had been strong allies of Osfrid. They and a number of other nobles had attended a meeting under a banner of truce. Tostig however, ordered their arrest and after a brief fight both of the men were executed. The next morning Tostig's men had arrived on Osfrid's land and warned him what would happen if he betrayed their lord.

The younger woman rolled her eyes, "Well if you hadn't noticed mother, we already are out of our home."

Aerlene felt a surge of anger at her daughter, but took a deep breath to calm herself. They were all scared, herself especially. She was full of worry for her husband, and as she looked to the horizon and saw the town ablaze, that feeling only deepened. She looked at her children. Their miserable faces and their shivering against the cold, tore at her heart.

They had accompanied Osfrid on his trip to the town at the request of the bishop; Wulf was not yet christened and today was the day he was supposed to become one of the Lords children. She was a devout Christian, but Osfrid still held his beliefs in the old religion, she had argued for hours until he finally relented and made the arrangements with the Bishop.

She had to do something. She walked to the edge of the stream and scooped up some of the icy cold water and splashed her face with it. The sensation of the dirt and muck washing away from her skin revitalised her, renewing her determination. She had faith in her husband; he had never let them down before.

"Your father said that if he did not meet us before Sunset, then we must head south towards Driffield and our own lands. Hopefully your father will make his way back to us." Aerlene said as she urged her children to start walking. Already the sun was starting to go down in the West.

With one last look at the burning city she said a prayer to God that the Lord would keep her husband safe.

***

3.

The prisoners had been walking all night; weariness had taken its toll on many of them. The moon was high and bright, giving the marching men plenty of light to move by.

The rolling foothills of the countryside were occasionally broken by steeper inclines and streams.

Hours passed as they trudged across fields, and passed through small settlements, the inhabitants awakened and scared by the passing soldiers.

Up ahead Osfrid could just make out Tostig riding on a horse, his hands bound to the saddle. Alongside him rode Cearl and a number of other Thegns.

Those that fell from exhaustion were speared by the following soldiers. The victorious troop's laughed again, indicating another death in the dark. Each time he heard it Osfrid winced in sympathy.

So far he had been treated well by his captors; Thegn Cearl had promised him his protection due to a favour he owed Osfrid's uncle.

Just as weariness threatened to overwhelm him the order to stop for the night was given. He sighed in relief as he slumped heavily to the ground. All around him the other prisoners did the same.

Several warriors rounded up the prisoners and forced them all to move into a nearby abandoned cattle pen. Several guards took position outside of the pen whilst others began to light campfires.

Within the hour the area was filled with the sounds of a victorious army. Drunken songs and tales of bravado echoed across the hills. However Osfrid was unaware of the commotion. As soon as he lay down he drifted off into a restless, haunted sleep full of concern for the days to come and, for his family.

***

4.

October 1065

Doncaster- South of York

Osfrid awoke to the sounds of a camp preparing to move on. All around, canvas tents and equipment were being taken down and loaded onto ox-drawn carts. The sky was filled with tumultuous grey clouds giving the dawn a dank and depressing feel. The sun was doing its best to break through the heavy cloud cover but to no avail.

"Morning milord", came a voice from his left. For a moment he forgot where he was, but as he looked around, the memories of the past day came flooding back into his tired brain. He could see he was in a small cattle pen, most likely to have been used to shelter a nearby grazing herd of sheep. The ground was wet and the aroma of animal faeces wafted into his nostrils.

Around him and huddled together were ten other prisoners. Some he recognised as Tostig's guards but others he assumed were villagers or servants caught up in the fighting.

He looked to see who had spoken and saw it was a man no older than eighteen summers. A short black beard adorned his face, and his face was pocked with scars, most likely from some illness he had suffered from in the past. Earnest brown eyes belied a sharp intelligence and quick wit not often seen in a town guard.

"Do you know where we are? Osfrid asked, as he watched a group of warriors folding up their tents and fastening saddles to their mounts.

"I overheard one of the guards say we were at the outskirts of Doncaster. We marched down the old Roman road all night to get here", the younger man replied.

"My name is Acca Cenersen; I was a guard at the barracks." He looked away at the mention of his former post. The town's barracks were attacked first by Morcar's forces and the fighting there had been brutal. Osfrid had seen firsthand the violence of the struggle as he had scouted the area earlier that day.

"You must have fought well to have lived Acca," He said as he stood up and wiped the mud from his sodden breaches. He stretched his aching muscles by touching his toes and rolling his shoulders. He grunted in satisfaction when he heard them crack.

"Aye sir I did, I skewered three of the bastards onto the end of my spear." Acca laughed proudly before frowning, as he remembered the faces of the men he'd killed. The prisoners settled into an awkward silence as they waited to see what their captors would do with them.

The early morning gave way to mid afternoon and still the camp was bustling with activity. A guard approached the cattle pen and threw in a loaf of dried bread which the prisoners greedily consumed.

"I remember seeing you at Tostig's hall," Acca said as he devoured the measly scrap of bread that he was stuffing into his mouth. Crumbs got caught in his beard in the process. "Were you a guard?"

Osfrid chuckled in amusement.

"If I were a guard then my life would be far simpler. No, I was no guard." He replied as he too bit into the stale bread.

"I figured as much, your armour is far too expensive for a guardsman to wear. So what was you doing there… if you don't mind me asking?"

Osfrid sighed deeply. The young man's questions were beginning to irritate him. After a brief pause he shrugged and told him why. It wouldn't matter.

"I was in York for the christening of my son. However, Tostig had other ideas and summoned me to him. It was whilst I was waiting for an audience, that the rioting broke out and Thegn Morcar's forces stormed the city."

Acca nodded as he heard his explanation. Just as he was about to ask another question a guard approached the pen and pulled open the gate. Under his arm he carried a sack; its contents clinking as he walked. The guard gestured to

Osfrid and told him to stand up. Tentatively Osfrid rose to his feet and cautiously approached his captor.

“Thegn Osfrid.’ the guard said. “Thegn Cearl has ordered your release. You are to accompany me to him.” The guard opened the sack and tipped its contents onto the ground. With a heavy thud Osfrid’s chainmail hauberk and chausses fell into the mud.

"A Thegn!"Acca's whispered excitement could be heard clearly by Osfrid. "My lord," he spoke with a clear and calm voice to Osfrid standing as straight as he could. "If you ever have need for a strong spear and an honest eye..." His eyes said the rest as Osfrid glanced at him. Osfrid knew exactly what he wished but turned and walked off without giving a hint of acknowledging the man.

“What of my weapons?” Osfrid growled as he lifted the mail shirt over his head and fastened it into position; flecks of mud covered the intricately linked metal rings. He would have given anything to have his sword in his hand and teach the guard a lesson for soiling his precious armour.

The guard smirked through his thick beard as he escorted Osfrid out of the pen and shut the gate behind him. As they headed further into the camp Acca’s pleas faded into the mix of the surrounding sounds of a busy camp.

“The Thegn has them’, the guard said. “They are quite safe.” He added reluctantly as Cearl came bounding into view.

In the daylight, and now that he was not concentrating on fighting for his life, Osfrid was able to measure up the man who had led the attack on Tostig's hall.

Cearl was a tall and broad shouldered man, for someone in their forties, he looked surprisingly fit and healthy. He wore his thinning on top black hair in a pony tail that reached to his shoulders and wore a long woollen cloak above his armour. Dirt covered his face making it evident that he had not washed since the fire in Tostig's hall.

"Osfrid Hunweldsen we meet again", The Thegn greeted cheerfully, making Osfrid instantly curious and suspicious of the man.

"Thegn Cearl", he greeted in return.

"I apologise for keeping you imprisoned for so long. Morcar and the others were so busy planning our next move that I am afraid to say I forgot about you", Cearl explained leading the way through the now dismantled camp. "I kept my word on keeping you safe though. I owe your uncle that much, the old whoreson saved my life during a Welsh attack about ten years ago", He explained as they passed a number of warriors preparing weapons and shepherding prisoners.

"My uncle was a drunk and a reckless bastard who got himself killed in a tavern brawl. I never liked the man, he was a fool, but I cannot deny he was good in a fight", replied Osfrid, he itched to hold his sword.

Cearl chuckled in agreement.

"Why did you release me? I fought your men, and killed your nephew", Osfrid murmured. He felt uneasy at Cearl's friendliness; the man had no reason to show him kindness. Cearl stopped walking and turned to face him. A look of irritation appeared on his features. A moment passed before he spoke.

"I released you, because you are a Thegn Osfrid. You are of noble blood, like me, and like Morcar", He said earnestly. "I know you were allies of Ulf and the others who opposed Tostig. I know that he must have threatened you greatly for you to serve the man you hate above all others."

"He threatened to rape my daughter, to murder my wife and son, to burn us out of our home and put Driffield to the sword" Osfrid said, barely able to contain his rage at the memory of Tostig's threat. The fear he had seen in the eyes of his wife had made him feel ashamed, ashamed of the fact that he wasn't strong enough to defy Tostig, or to defend his land. Often he had thought about raising his Fyrd and marching on York himself.

As a Thegn he was able to call a hundred men to battle and fight for the king in times of need, but such daydreams were a futile wish. Tostig commanded many more men and any confrontation would have led to a massacre.

As they walked a thought occurred to him.

"I've often thought about doing what you and Morcar have done, but surely once the king learns of what has taken place, he will declare you outlaws. You risk civil war."

Finally they reached a large tent, its banner wafting gently in the cold autumn breeze.

Cearl stopped, "This is Morcar's tent. He has summoned every Thegn in the north to him. Now we will decide our next course of action. Don't worry about the King, Osfrid. After we explain our actions he will understand our reasons for it. Now come inside, Morcar wants to speak with you." With that, Cearl opened the flap and ushered Osfrid inside.

Inside the spacious tent was a pallet and a solitary stool, upon which sat a man; a jug of water was on the ground at his feet.

He was Morcar; the large squat man was instantly recognisable. A thick black beard covered his face and he wore a leather cap to cover his bald head. Intelligence radiated out of his grey eyes and Osfrid knew he would be a difficult man to deceive.

"You must be Thegn Osfrid", Morcar said in a deep grave voice. He rose from the stool and grasped Osfrid strongly by the arm, a look of regret on his face. "I am sorry at the way you were treated", he said, "If I had known who you were I would have had you released sooner", He added apologetically.

"No harm has been done Thegn Morcar. I am just happy to be free and alive", said Osfrid as he took the jug of water and drank from it. The cool water sated his thirst and restored some strength into his aching limbs.

The big man looked at Osfrid with interest. He had heard of the man's uncle and his father. Both men had been mighty warriors in their day, and from what Cearl had told him, the man standing before him was of the same mould.

Osfrid took another sip of water before asking, "What will you do if the King doesn't take your side in this? The Godwinson's are the most powerful family in the kingdom. Harold will not take the news of his brother's capture lightly."

Morcar nodded his head in agreement. "Aye, Tostig will petition to Harold to have him freed and if he succeeds, his vengeance will be brutal. But Harold is no fool, and I have heard that his patience is running thin when it comes to the actions of his brother."

"I hope to god that what you say is true. If not then it will be my family and the people of York that will pay the price", Osfrid said worriedly.

Morcar stood up from the stool and began to pace the floor. His thick set features were knotted in thought. After a few moments he stopped and looked at Osfrid, a glint was in his eye.

"Come with me Osfrid, and tell of Tostig's cruelty and threats to Harold. Face to face. If he hears the accusations from enough of the Thegn's he will have no other option but to take our side."

Osfrid sighed heavily. What Morcar was proposing was a risky endeavour. If the King chose in favour of Tostig then he could lose everything to the tyrant's petty cruelty. His thoughts went to his wife and children, who he was sure, would have headed to Driffield after he failed to arrive at the meeting place they'd agreed upon.

As he thought of his wife, her beautiful long dark auburn hair and large brown eyes, full of love for him. He realised that it would be foolish to pass up the chance that Morcar had given him. He didn't agree with the man's actions, after all what he had done could be seen as an act of war against the king, But, if the king did agree then there was a chance he could be free of Tostig forever. His family and lands would be safe, at least for the near future.

"I will go with you Morcar. Any chance to rid myself of Tostig must be taken."

Morcar smiled and then laughed in delight.

"Excellent! With your testimony, and that of the others, we will be rid of that devil forever. Come Osfrid, I will get someone to return your weapons and get you a new horse."

Osfrid held up his hands to stall Morcar.

"Before we leave I must send word to Driffield and let my wife know that I am safe. I would never hear the end of it otherwise, especially if I left with you and was killed by Harold", He joked.

He would need to send someone with a message and tried to think of someone to take it. His thoughts went back to the man he had spoken with in the cattle pen.

"I want the man Acca to be released from the cattle pen where I was held. He can take the message for me. He seemed honest enough to be trustworthy", He explained.

"Very well, I'll see to his release. Now if you don't mind my new friend, I have an army to move. I sent messengers south last night to inform the king of what has transpired. We will march to Bicester and wait for a response. It will take a good few days to make the journey. Go and see Cearl to get your provisions."

Osfrid nodded and left the tent, he had a long march ahead of him.

***

5.

October 1065

Royal palace Westminster,

London

The rider had galloped all through the night and his stamina was waning. Sweat dampened his forehead. He could still feel the autumn cold through his black cloak, but despite that, the haste of his journey made him feel exhausted.

Up ahead in the distance on the banks of the river Thames was the stone palace of King Edward. It was a marvel to behold, its stone tower stood high and proud over the nearby town. Only the magnificent abbey next to it came close to matching its size in the entire realm.

A flock of seagulls flew overhead, their shrill calls echoing across the marshy plain. The sun was only just rising in the east casting its orange glow over the countryside. Any other time he would have stopped to admire the view but the information he was carrying couldn't wait another moment.

With a cry he spurred his tired horse onwards towards the royal abode. After a ten minute gallop the rider crossed the wooden bridge that led into London proper. Thatched roof houses numbered in their hundreds, and the muddy streets were filled with people getting up to start their day. Butchers and other merchants were beginning to set up their market stalls, and put out their stock for potential customers. The messenger swore as he was delayed by a merchants cart blocking the narrow street. After threatening and cajoling the merchant he was able to get it moved. But precious moments were wasted.

Eventually he reached the palaces gate house. He took out his royal seal and showed it to the Huscarl's guarding the entrance. They waved him on through. As he approached the stables he called for a stable boy to take his horses reins. Quickly he dismounted, as a small scruffy boy ran out to take the horse's reins and led it away to be fed and watered.

The large wooden doors opened with a creak as he approached. Two guards stepped forward to challenge him but once more the messenger flashed his seal. They waved him in and ushered him down a long hallway. Stain-glass windows sat high on the walls and a number of flaming braziers lit the route. At intervals down the hall stood armoured Huscarl's, vigilant as always to any dangers the king might face.

After a long walk he reached a large chamber. The walls were covered in beautiful tapestries depicting the images of past kings and queens. The flickering light from the braziers cast an eerie glow giving the images an ethereal appearance.

A large stone altar dominated the centre of the chamber, upon which an ornately decorated crucifix stood in glory. A plethora of gems and other valuable stones adorned its solid gold surface. The messenger paused at the sights before him; this was one chamber he had never been sent to before.

Finally his eyes settled on the figure of a man knelt in prayer at the foot of the altar. Only the golden circlet sat upon the man's head and almost hidden by his shoulder length greying hair indicated that this was King Edward.

Most people assumed that the king was always adorned in jewels and fine clothes but for Edward this was not the case. He scorned such things and instead devoted himself to living a life of simplicity in the name of god. The king had always been a deeply pious man, but ever since the onset of his illness, and rapidly deteriorating health, he had spent most of his time in the chapel and at prayer. Whispers abounded that it was Harold Godwinson that in fact ran the kingdom's affairs.

"My lord King?" the messenger spoke nervously. He cringed as his voice broke the holy silence.

A fit of violent coughing emanated from the king in response. At once an attendant hurried to his side carrying a cloth and bowel. The messenger looked away as Edward coughed up phlegm and blood.

Eventually with the attendants help the king rose from his knees and turned to face the messenger. Despite his pale face, a forehead covered by sweat and his features strained the king's voice was still strong and clear. The king's gaunt white face gave him the appearance of a man on the verge of entering heaven.

"What news do you bring me from the North?"

"My lord, I bring grave tidings. A rebellion has occurred in York. The town was sacked and reports are that at least two hundred souls were slain. Dozens of Thegn's led by Morcar of Northumbria attacked the town and have captured Tostig Godwinson. He leads an army a thousand strong and has requested a meeting with you to pass judgement upon him. They claim Earl Tostig was a tyrant and a traitor", the messenger said carefully.

Anger flashed across the kings features. He waved off the attendant who was steadying him and with a visible effort walked to the altar, and placed his hands on either side of the golden cross.

"Who are they to take such actions? How dare they do this! Only I and almighty god have the right to depose a Thegn!" Edward shouted in a high pitched rage. His voice echoed around the chapel.

Many of his subjects mocked the king behind his back, he still sounded like an unbroken youth whose voice would rise like a girl's when stressed.

After a while and once his fit ended, he composed himself and summoned his attendant.

"Bring Lord Harold to me! I must discuss this with him." Anger threatened to spill out of him but he kept his voice low, his bottom lip trembling. With a bow the attendant left and with a dismissive gesture from the king, the messenger who had travelled for three days straight bowed and left--unpaid.

***

Harold Godwinson laughed in delight as he watched the stag fall to his spear throw. It had been a hard and long hunt but finally he had his prize. He reigned in his white horse and ordered the servants to fetch the animal's carcass from the thick undergrowth.

"A fine kill my lord", one of the Norman dignitaries praised. Harold flashed him a boyish grin and spurred his horse deeper into the woods.

At forty three years of age he was no longer the youth with infinite energy he once was but he still loved to hunt, the thrill of the chase never grew tiresome.

He was tall and towered over most men, his good looks making him instantly popular with the fairer sex. His fine green woollen cloak was splattered with mud caused by the horses galloping through the damp forest undergrowth and his boots were filthy but despite his appearance he still looked regal.

He had risen to fame and glory after his campaign against the Welsh two years previously and was the King's right hand man. His ambition however extended beyond this role, he wanted the crown after the sickly Edward passed over but knew he had rivals to succeed him as king.

His father had been the most powerful earl in the kingdom and Harold had surpassed even him. Despite his father, the King's past quarrels and his family's resulting exile the

Godwinsons had returned to become more powerful than ever.

Looking around him he watched as three of the Norman dignitaries laughed and joked. Those men represented the face of one of those competitors, William Duke of Normandy. Ever since his capture after being shipwrecked on the Norman coast a few years previously, Harold had pretended to be friends with the Duke. At the time of his capture he had made promises in order to save his own skin, even going as far as being made a knight in William's court. Now here he was trying to keep up the deception by entertaining the Duke's ambassadors. His thoughts drifted back to those fearful days and he regretted the oaths he had pledged to William, oaths that he would have to break to achieve his own ambitions.

The sun was beginning to set and dusk wasn't far off. Hunting in the woods of his Wiltshire estate at night was dangerous thanks to the wolves that roamed the area. With a reluctant sigh he gave the signal to his squire to call an end to the day's proceedings. The body of the stag he had killed was lifted onto the back of a pony which was laden with the corpses of other successful kills. A number of birds, a fox and two deer were the day's bounty and all would make fine trophies or dinner.

The hunting party left the woods and started along the dirt track that would take them back to London. They were met halfway by a messenger.

"Lord Godwinson, the king wishes to see you at once. Grave news has come from the North."

Harold frowned and apologised to the others in the hunting group that he had to leave them. He spurred his horse into a gallop and together with the messenger sped towards London and the King's news.

***

6.

October 1065

Driffield

The road to Driffield wound through the Yorkshire countryside. The chill of autumn was now beginning to succeed the hastily departing warmth of the summer. Wind swept across the dales in a high pitched howl that made Acca think the element itself was alive.

He wrapped his cloak tighter around his body, trying his best not to be buffeted by the cold air. Dressed in only a thin woollen shirt and leather hose he shivered violently in the saddle. At least he had been allowed to take a horse for the journey; he grimaced at the thought of having to walk all the way there.

The horse whinnied and bucked as a rabbit darted across the muddy road in front of him. It was an old nag of a horse, but Acca didn't mind. He had never been much of a horseman.

When the Thegn Osfrid had requested he be released, he was delighted, but now after enduring this long journey he wished he'd not been so earnest in his pleas for freedom.

He shook his head, "No. I am a loyal man," he said out loud. After all, his father had always said; *'no matter what hardships are thrown at you Acca, always be loyal to those around you'*.

Acca smiled at the memory of his father. He had been a good and honest man, who had done well by his wife and ten children. Sadly, he had died of the pox several winters previously leaving Acca the head of the household.

With little knowledge of farming Acca had enlisted with the York guard and sent what meagre earnings he made to his mother and siblings who lived on a scraggy piece of farm land several miles away from the city.

The last piece of news he had heard from them was that they were all doing fine, in a letter his sister had wrote, it had said that two of his brothers had joined the Huscarl's of a local Thegn, and that one of his sisters was to be wed to a local merchant. The fact that he could read at all was a miracle. His father had worked tirelessly to pay for a basic education for his brood. Acca had the opportunity to join the church as a monk or scholar but to him the call of the sword and adventure had been too enticing.

Even the darkening sky and increasing winds couldn't dampen his pride at the memories.

Acca was brought out of his revelry as he crested a small hill and saw before him a wide valley with a grove of apple trees on each side of the slanting slopes. Their fruit was no longer the golden or red colour that one would have seen in the summer, they were brown and rotting as the season's first frosts attacked them.

He squinted his eyes, and could just make out plumes of wood smoke amongst the trees and the grey sky.

"This must be Driffield" he said jovially, happy to have finally reached his destination and the promise of the warmth of a raging fire.

He dug his heels into his horse and spurred the gelding into a trot that quickly took him down into the orchards and eventually into a wide clearing. Five mud and thatch huts stood in a semi circle at one side and at the other stood several wooden market stools and what looked like an ale house. Some goats were in a pen next to a sturdy looking stone cottage and the sound of chickens could clearly be heard. A narrow stream divided the settlement in two with a small footbridge spanning the gap. On the opposite side of the stream a dozen more huts could be seen, a small lad was chasing chickens and a blacksmith was shoeing a mule.

Acca licked his lips at the thought of drinking himself into oblivion next to a warm cozy fire. He looked around and could hear laughter coming from within the ale house, it sounded like some sort of celebration was going on. Curious he dismounted his horse and taking the reins walked towards the inn. He tied his horse securely to a cracked and gnarled wooden post before entering.

The place was dimly lit, only the fire place which he longed to warm himself by and a few candles lit the interior. A long oak bar ran along the back wall, a dozen barrels of ale stacked up in one corner. Hunting trophies adorned the walls, Acca could see two stags heads and one boars affixed to pedestals hanging from nails.

As he took in his new surroundings he noticed that the laughter he had heard previously had been replaced by a nervous mutter. He could see the bars patrons staring at him, looks of uncertainty and curiosity adorning their faces. Just as he was about to introduce himself a man emerged from a backroom behind the bar. He was in his forties with a balding head that was still struggling to hold onto the few remaining strands of whitish hair. His face was flushed red, the sign of a lifelong ale drinker and his massive stomach threatened to burst from his breaches.

"Who are you?" the barman asked after a moment of awkward silence.

"My name is Acca I have a message to deliver to the Thegn of Driffield's hall" Acca replied slowly as he noticed many of the bars patrons leaning in to overhear the conversation.

The fat man scowled and glanced around at the patrons. "Thegn Osfrid you mean?"

"Yes, yes Thegn Osfrid, I promised him that I would send word to his family that he still lives" He replied earnestly.

The locals behaviour was starting to unsettle him, although he shouldn't be surprised he thought. Most small settlements were cautious around strangers.

Another man's voice came from the rear of the ale house drowning out the muttering from the other patrons who had began talking fervently amongst themselves upon hearing Acca speak.

"I will take you to Osfrid's hall lad."

Acca turned to see a man walking towards him. He was tall and had a fine head of blond hair and a long plaited beard. The man wore a tunic of green and brown and was carrying a large battleaxe in his hands. The man eyed up Acca and after a brief moment of studying him he smiled and slung the axe over his left shoulder and offered his hand.

"My name is Ceadda. I am the captain of Thegn Osfrid's Fyrd and steward of his hall"

Acca cautiously shook the man's hand. Something was amiss he could feel it.

"I apologise Ceadda but I was told to give this message directly to the Thegn's wife."

A confused look crossed Ceadda's face.

"Lady Aerlene? But she has not returned to Driffield. We thought that she and Thegn Osfrid would be in York until the end of the month."

Acca took a step backwards in shock. How could Osfrid's wife not be here? A sense of dread began to knot in his stomach. Ceadda took Acca by the arm and led him back outside into the cold autumn air.

"Tell me all that you know boy." He demanded.

"There was a rebellion in York by the Thegn's and Tostig was captured. Osfrid too was taken prisoner along with me during the fighting, but he was released once his identity was discovered." He began to pace the floor as he explained what had happened. Ceadda paled as he heard the tale.

"Tostig was captured? That man swore bloody vengeance upon this place and upon our Thegn. Could it be some of his men would have taken lady Aerlene and the children?"

Acca looked at Ceadda in horror. "We must find them!" he shouted, "They cannot be far, it would be near impossible for one of Tostig's men to reach this place faster than I. They would have only a day's head start on us." he explained as he raced towards his horse.

He launched himself into the saddle and was about to race off towards Osfrid's hall when Ceadda called to him.

"What good do you think you'll do without a weapon lad?"

Acca stared at the man dumbfounded for a few seconds before he realised he was indeed unarmed, his sword and spear had been taken by Morcar's men during the assault on York. Before he could reply Ceadda walked over to his own mount and reached into the saddle bags.

After a quick rummage the big man pulled out a sword. The blades hilt was plain iron and the blade itself looked old and chipped. After examining it Ceadda grunted in satisfaction and tossed the weapon to the now mounted Acca, who caught it nimbly by the pommel.

"It may not be the grandest looking of swords lad but in its day my granddaddy killed his fair share of Danes with It." boasted the elder man proudly. He strapped his battle axe to his saddle and mounted his own grey horse and gestured for Acca to follow, before long the two of them were riding hard towards Osfrid's hall.

Hedgerows and fields sped by and on more than one occasion farmers in the fields called out greetings to Ceadda. The big man yelled at them to hasten to their Thegn's hall as soon as they were able and to spread the word amongst the local populace.

"The word will spread, and the Fyrd will form. Hopefully we will have over a hundred men to help in finding lady Aerlene and the children by the morning." Ceadda explained over the noise of galloping hooves and the horse's heavy breathing.

Worry knotted around Acca's guts like an insidious serpent. He had made an oath to Osfrid and he would not rest until he had delivered his message to the Thegn's wife, even if that meant searching until the end of the world.

"We may not have that long." Acca said as he ducked under a low branch, "we may just be thinking the worst, perhaps the lady Aerlene has been delayed." He added optimistically.

Ceadda frowned; "When it comes to that bastard Tostig, it pays to be cautious. He killed my brother for sport after making false accusations against him. It's a good thing he's been deposed but when it comes to Osfrid he would go to the devil himself to take revenge" He could barely contain his anger as he spoke.

Finally they reached a narrow river with a steep incline on the opposite bank; there sat upon it was Driffield hall. Its large wooden walls hid the manor house from view but a watchtower could be seen looking outwards towards the eastern coastline.

The days of Viking raids and invasions was in the past, but those who lived near the sea still kept a vigilant watch on the horizon for the sails of Viking longboats.

Ceadda pointed to a rickety looking bridge further down the river and the two men spurred their horses towards it. After galloping across the river they were now in a flat patch of land with the hill in which the hall sat to their left. The open ground they crossed to reach the base of the hill was a killing space that would enable defenders to form a shield wall and attack any besieging enemy force.

The hill wasn't as steep as Acca had first thought as they approached the gates, probably due to the front gate being the only way in or out of the palisade. Ceadda hailed a guard who promptly banged his spear onto the gates surface. After a brief wait the gate creaked open and the two men rode inside. Unlike most Thegns' halls Osfrid's had a distinctly military feel to it. It was built more like a fort than a landowner's home.

"Osfrid's father Hunweld was a warrior through and through, he couldn't rest until he knew his home was well protected" Ceadda explained as they dismounted, and waited for a boy to take their horses to the stable at the far end of the fort. "This place can shelter over twenty families and always has enough grain in its stores to last for several months."

"Sounds like he was constantly prepared for war" Acca said as he took in his surroundings.

"He was, and with good reason. Hunweld never believed the king to be strong enough to protect his people; before he left for the East he made Osfrid promise that Driffield would always stand strong, and it has." Ceadda replied proudly. "At least until lately, Tostig has done his best to weaken us."

Ceadda led the way inside the main hall.

It was similar to others Acca had been in, it had high walls and was strongly built with a thatch and pitch roof. Thick oak beams crisscrossed the ceiling ensuring that even the strongest of winter storms wouldn't be able to topple it. A large open fireplace that was currently unlit dominated one wall. A long dining table was against another. On the floor lay a carpet of furs and animal skins and there was a ladder leading to the families' living space above the far end wall. The main thing different that he noticed were all of the strange and exotic items adorning the walls, Strange curved swords and pieces of artwork, the likes of which he'd never seen before.

He stepped closer to what appeared to be a banner of some sort. Adorning it was a mighty eagle of gold upon a deep purple background. Emblazoned around it were words written in a strange language that he couldn't understand.

"It's from the East lad, and it's from a very long time ago." Ceadda said as he stood next to Acca and looked up at the eagle. "Osfrid's father left for the East ten years ago and from time to time he sends back these strange things. Apparently this was a banner once carried by the armies of Rome as they conquered the Eastern lands."

"The Thegn's father is alive?" asked Acca confused; he thought that only the head of the family could bear the title of Thegn.

"Aye he's alive. He left the title to Osfrid with the kings blessing. I think the king was secretly glad to be rid of Hunweld; he was strongly opposed to the king's friends in Normandy.

The last we heard of the scoundrel was two years ago, apparently he's living in Constantinople and doing very well for himself."

Acca looked at the exotic objects in awe. Constantinople was like a myth to him, he had heard tales of the golden city and the remnants of the Roman Empire.

Ceadda gestured to the banner. "It says Quae caret ora cruore nostro?'

Which is Latin for, what coast knows not our blood? It makes you think ay lad."

The elder man told Acca to rest while he gathered his men. Acca just nodded never before had he seen such wondrous things, his head filled with dreams of travel and seeing the wonders of the world.

For several hours he just stood and looked at the objects before Ceadda brought him a drink of goat's milk and a plate of bread and ham.

"Eat up lad; you'll need to keep your strength up for tomorrow." He said as he sat at the long table. "While you were resting I had some of my men find out what they could about lady Aerlene's location."

"What did you find out?" Acca asked hopefully through a mouthful of cheese.

Ceadda sighed before downing the rest of his cup of beer.

"We were right to be cautious my young friend. One of my men was out on the moors yesterday, said that he spotted a small band of horsemen travelling northwards. Amongst them were two women and a boy."

Acca jumped up from his stool and reached for the sword that was resting on the floor at his feet. "That has to be them." He said excitedly.

Ceadda put a hand on Acca's shoulder. "It does sound like it but we must not rush off to find them. Night will fall soon and we don't want to be caught out in it. Bandits and other fell creatures lurk on the moors when the sun goes down." He made the sign of the cross before walking over to the open fire and threw a fresh log into the inferno. Sparks erupted as the fire was reenergized by this fresh source of fuel. Shadows leapt up across the walls giving the hall an eerie atmosphere. "We will start the search at first light. We'll have the Fyrd with us then so we can cover a lot more ground. Get some sleep Acca; you can stay in one of the out buildings tonight."

Acca nodded, all his thoughts were now focused on the day to come and what was sure to be a difficult search. He had made a promise to Osfrid. And he never broke his promises.

***

7.

Esma almost smiled as she watched her mother give their captor an almighty slap across his ugly scarred face. The man's head visibly rocked backwards at the impact causing him to stagger backwards in a daze. He'd had it coming for a while. The man had a shaven head and a face that was a criss-cross of scars old and new. One thing Esma's mother couldn't stand was a leering lecherous man. However her mirth turned to fear as the bald man recovered his wits and snarled in anger.

"Bloody bitch!" he shouted as he brought his fist across Aerlene's face with a backhanded punch. Esma screamed as her mother was sent sprawling to the ground. Mud now covered her from head to toe, her dress was torn and blood flowed from her nose.

Esma had discovered a new found respect for her mother as she watched her shakily get back onto her feet and glare at the man, her dark brown eyes filled with anger and defiance. Esma's little brother buried his head into her skirts and silently sobbed, much as he had done all throughout their terrible ordeal.

"Be strong little Wulf, father will find us and save us", She whispered comfortingly to him.

The man raised his arm to her mother once more but halted when another man grabbed it and threw him to the ground. He put his knee onto the bald mans throat and growled;

"You sniffling little bastard, our orders are to take this lot to the border unharmed. Tostig wants to deal with them himself, and here you are trying to rob his lordship of his pleasure."

Esma ran to her mother and hugged her tightly; Wulf clung onto the both of them. Aerlene protectively stood between her children and the two men who had taken them captive the day before. After the fall of York she had taken the children towards Driffield, they had been only hours away from home before the men caught up to them.

The two men were obviously mercenaries, neither looked as though they belonged to a professional army. Each wore a leather jerkin and boots but their underclothes were filthy and no doubt lice ridden.

Handel was the name of the leader and the one who was now beating his compatriot to a pulp. He too had a shaved head but his defining feature was long black beard that stretched almost to his waist. Strips of cloth were wrapped around small bones which were braided throughout the coarse hair. He had boasted to Wulf that they were the bones of the little children he had eaten. The scarred man was a Dane called Gulbrandr.

Handel delivered a swift kick to Gulbrandr's nether regions and spat on the ground as he turned to face the terrified family.

"Filthy Dane he is. He'd rut with his own horse if he could, the dirty bastard, Apologies my lady." he said sarcastically giving a patronising curtsey.

"What do you want with us?" shouted Esma, her anger and fear threatened to boil over. She was petrified that she would be the Danes next target; he had been eyeing her up all day. Aerlene shushed her daughter and put an arm around her.

"Thegn Tostig is going to pay me and my friend here a lot of money for you. He wanted your husband too." Handel replied as he dragged his now unconscious colleague towards the tied up horses.

They too would not travel at night fearing the dales and moors when it got dark. Instead they set up a small camp in a clearing at the side of the road. A grove of trees and bushes offered some protection from the elements and had provided enough fuel for a camp fire, which was a necessity against the plummeting temperatures.

"Tostig could have killed my husband in York on many occasions, why would he pay you to do it?" Aerlene asked, genuinely curious.

She knew about the rivalry between her husband and Tostig. Many times their land had been threatened, but it wasn't until Osfrid's friends and sworn brothers took a stand against Tostig's increasingly tyrannical behaviour that they had been threatened with death. The night Osfrid's friends had been murdered was the night when

Osfrid began to sleep with his sword close to the bed and doubled the watch on the walls at Driffield.

"Tostig knew someone would rise against him and he wanted to strike back at those who did. He never trusted your husband, even though he made him swear an oath to defend him. How that must've killed your hubby, swearing to protect his hated enemy or else have his family killed" Handel laughed menacingly. "And now that York has fallen to Morcar, Tostig has unleashed us and others like us to strike at his enemies families. Ya see York was our signal to start having a little fun."

Aerlene stared at Handel in shock, aghast at how conniving and twisted Tostig had become. To be so paranoid as to have men ready to strike at a possible foes family was beyond her imaginings.

"Were taking you to Scotland where our lord has many friends, who knows he may let you live as slaves if you're lucky." Handel cackled as he unfurled a bedroll onto the ground. He lay down and took out a lethal looking dagger which he then preceded to stroke. He looked at the family menacingly.

"I suggest you get some rest, we've a long journey tomorrow. Oh, and no funny business I'm a very light sleeper and I'll gut you like a fish if you try to run."

Aerlene nodded in understanding. She glanced at the Dane who had now recovered from his beating and was now sat up and staring at them. His vicious expression sent a shiver down her spine as she and the children found a place to lie down under a tree. She brought the children closer to her and embraced them tightly to keep in some warmth.

An hour past and the moon emerged from the clouds casting its magnificent light onto the moors. Nocturnal animals could be heard scurrying about the undergrowth and the shriek of an owl echoed across the hills in the distance.

Both of the children had fallen asleep due to their exhaustion of the past day. She reached into her cloak and pulled out one of her daughters hair pins. It was bronze and decorated in the shape of an eagle. She glanced over at her sleeping captors and hurled the pin out into the darkness. She made a silent prayer asking god for deliverance before falling into a restless sleep.

***

8.

October 1065

Northampton

Osfrid paced nervously as he waited. Word had reached them from the south that King Edward had ordered Harold Godwinson to march his army to meet them before they reached London. England was on the brink of civil war and it was all down to the men he now found himself travelling with. He stopped his pacing as he saw Cearl and Morcar's brother, Edwin the Earl of Mercia ride through the camp towards Morcar's command tent. Osfrid had known the Earl for years and had fought alongside him on many occasions against the Welsh and Scots. He was a man with a dry sense of humour and would often turn a serious situation into a light hearted affair.

A week had almost passed since the sacking of York and as the rebel force had marched southwards, more and more Thegn's had thrown in their support for Morcar.

To Osfrid's distaste the army had sacked and pillaged as they went, Lincoln, Derby and Nottingham had all been put to the sword. His complaints about the resulting slaughter had fallen on deaf ears. Morcar argued that they were towns loyal to Tostig and had to be removed, a view that many of the other Thegn's agreed with.

Osfrid however had not taken part in the attacks but had instead led a group of Huscarl's to assist escaping refugees. On more than one occasion he had had to draw his sword on drunken rampaging soldiers threatening innocent and terrified people.

He had seen the brutality of war many times but nothing prepared him for the ruthlessness and brutality that had been inflicted upon the town of Northampton.

The army had reached the town two days previously and had demanded that the town provide provisions and shelter. The town leaders had refused, claiming that Morcar was a rebel and an outlaw.

At this, Morcar had flown into a rage and had stormed the town, his men had raped and pillaged for an entire day and night.

The arrival of Earl Edwin and his force of Welsh mercenaries had not helped matters. It took another day before Osfrid and Cearl could restore order to the army.

He looked down from his vantage point atop a hill and looked towards the walled and broken town to the West; the beautiful spire of the nearby church dominated the skyline and sat amongst hundreds of wisps of smoke rising from the burning houses of the town.

It looked so peaceful and yet dreadful that it made him yearn to be back in Driffield with his family and away from the affairs of nobles and warlords. He longed for his father's return from the East so that he could pass back the reins of power and the responsibility to live a peaceful life.

The ground crunched as he turned and strode towards his horse that was grazing happily on a nearby patch of grass.

The temperature had plummeted overnight and frost was still present on the hard ground even though it was midday. He pulled his heavy woollen cloak tighter around him as a gust of icy wind swept across the camp and over the hill.

His thoughts drifted to the man he had saved from imprisonment and a small twang of doubt crossed his mind. Surely the lad had delivered his message by now? If so then why had he not received word from home that his family was safe? He shook his head to drive the worry from his heart; he couldn't be distracted, not now, not when the fate of his enemy and the kingdom was balancing on a razors edge. He grabbed the horse's reigns and whispered soothingly into the beast's ear. Hauling himself into the saddle he set off at a trot down the hill and into the camp below.

All around him soldiers were going about their work or just sat around drinking and eating. The banners of over fifty Thegn's fluttered in the wind and the sounds of blacksmiths sharpening weapons filled the air. The army that Morcar now led was almost eight thousand strong and with Earl Edwin's arrival that number had increased by another five hundred.

Never before had Osfrid seen so many of his countrymen and fellow warriors gathered in one place, it filled him with both a sense of pride and a feeling of dread.

A part of him felt that Morcar was being reckless. England was besieged by enemies abroad and they could ill afford to be fighting amongst themselves. Another part felt that York had been necessary. Tostig's tyrannical rule had to be ended and the king had to be shown that the earls and Thegn's would not allow themselves to be ruled by such a man.

Eventually he reached Morcar's tent and dismounted. A guardsman took the reins of his horse and took it to the nearby pen. Osfrid nodded his head in thanks and stepped inside. The tents layout was much the same way it had been when it was pitched just outside of York except this time he noticed a large pile of papers lying on top of a table.

Morcar was standing over an open parchment, his hands resting on the edges of the table; the big man was deep in thought as he read it. Cearl and Edwin were chatting casually to one side.

It was the first time Osfrid had seen the Earl in many years. The looks of youth were long faded and his once flowing locks of blonde hair had now turned a light grey. Like his brother he was large in stature and had a similar style of beard. Cearl was holding his helmet under his arm and smiled in greeting as he noticed Osfrid.

"Thegn Osfrid, It is good to see you my old friend." The earl greeted him warmly. The two men clasped arms in greeting.

"Indeed it has Edwin. I was just thinking, whose this old man I see before me." Osfrid replied lightly.

Cearl chuckled at Edwin's look of comedic outrage.

"Rude as ever I see." Edwin laughed. "How are things? How is your family?"

Osfrid brushed a hand through his long hair and noticed Morcar had taken Cearl aside and was whispering fervently with him. Osfrid frowned in curiosity.

"My family are well... At least they were the last time I saw them. Truth is told I want this situation resolved so I can get back to them as soon as possible."

"Aye we all want that my friend. But my brother's actions had to be taken; Tostig was a menace to all of our lands, including mine." Edwin replied as he poured himself a jug of wine. He offered Osfrid a cup which he accepted.

"So my brother what news have we from the South?" asked Edwin. The earl wore a heavy black cloak trimmed with wolf fur, giving him an imperious look. Compared to the other men in the room his clothing actually made him look as though he deserved his title.

Osfrid and the others were all wearing their chainmail armour and travel stained over clothes. He looked at his feet and noticed that his boots were caked with mud and filth. It had been days since he had even washed himself or been out of his mail since York. Since then they hadn't had very many opportunities to rest, time was of the essence.

After the march south and the sacking of several towns even sleep had been a rare commodity for the Thegn's. Keeping control of so many warriors and managing the logistics of such a journey had pushed them all to the edge.

Osfrid looked at Morcar and could see the weariness in his eyes, the man still had the steely gaze of defiance and determination but the dark rings and wrinkles betrayed his exhaustion. Very soon events would have to be settled.

"Harold marches to meet us. My scouts inform me that he will be arriving tomorrow." Morcar told his brother. For the first time since meeting him Osfrid saw a look of concern on the big man's features, he realised then that Morcar was afraid of Harold or at least was concerned about facing him in battle.

"How many men does he lead?" Edwin asked hastily. Fear was evident in his voice as well. Osfrid wondered if the two brothers had seriously thought they would be able to avoid facing the elder Godwinson. If so then the two of them were fools.

"He comes with just a dozen bodyguards." Morcar replied and once more filled his cup with wine.

Cearl looked at Osfrid and caught his eye, a look of guarded curiosity on his face. "It sounds like he's coming here to talk."

"It makes sense, I doubt he'd want to risk his brother's life by engaging us in battle and we must think ahead as well my brother." Edwin said as he now paced up and down. Morcar raised an eyebrow in curiosity.

"Edwards rule is failing, and it is well known that Harold has his eyes on the crown. He will need the support of the Northern earls and Thegn's for that ambition to be realised. He will surely bow to our demands in exchange for our backing."

Osfrid was mortified.

"So it is treason against the king, I suspected as much." He shouted in anger. "You swore to me this was about removing Tostig from power and not making a manoeuvre for the crown." It took all of his self control to not reach for his sword and strike down Morcar.

"Osfrid my friend" Edwin said soothingly as he put an arm around the Thegn's broad shoulders. "I assure you, we are not after the throne. We are simply being realistic, Tostig is favoured by Edward and the king is no doubt demanding all of our heads for the actions we have taken, even if it is for the good of the kingdom."

"None of us want war Osfrid." Cearl added reassuringly.

***

"Riders incoming" came a shout from the camps guards. Osfrid left his tent and stepped out into the bright morning sunshine. He raised an arm to shield his eyes from the dazzlingly bright sun. A clatter of hoofs signalled the arrival of a score of horsemen who swept into the centre of the camp. At their head was the unmistakable figure of Harold Godwinson. His arrival to Northampton would seal the fate of Osfrid's sworn enemy.

His face showed a serene certainty as he swept his gaze over the quickly assembling warriors. He rode a white horse that was richly bridled with polished leather and glittering silver. He wore brown leather boots, black breeches, a grey tunic and a gold trimmed green cloak while at his side hung a black-scabbard sword. Following behind him on their own mounts were a dozen fierce looking Huscarl's.

Each wore a coat of mail and carried a fearsome battle axe. They each took defensive positions around Harold and dismounted.

After a brief pause, an uneasy silence descended upon the camp and Harold stared at the warriors that had gathered to see him. Osfrid pushed his way through the crowds towards Cearl who was standing grim faced outside of Morcar's tent. He nodded to him in recognition as the cloth flap opened to reveal Morcar dressed in his mail armour, which had been polished until it shone in the autumn sunlight. Beside him stood Edwin who ushered a nervous looking monk out ahead of them. In his hands were a roll of parchment, a pot of ink and a quill which he was trying to balance precariously in his arms.

"He's here to record the meeting." Cearl whispered to Osfrid as the small group moved into the camp and onwards to meet Harold.

As they made their way through the camp groups of Thegn's and nobles joined them, each wanting to hear what Harold would say. Cearl strode on ahead and pushed his way through the gathered warriors barking orders as he went. Eventually the warriors made way for the nobles, either going back to their duties or standing back from the noblemen forming a circle around them at a respectful distance.

Harold glared at the Thegn's as they approached. Anger simmered under the surface of his conscience. Finally as the rebel nobles gathered in front of him he dismounted his horse. A Housecarl stepped forward and took the reigns as the others formed a defensive line behind and to the side of their master. Any assassin would be cut down before he'd even have a chance to draw a blade.

Morcar and Edwin stepped forward and bowed slightly in respect. As the two most powerful rebel nobles they would lead this encounter, a fact that made Osfrid uneasy. He rested a hand on his sword hilt, tense and ready for anything.

A strained silence descended over them before Harold calmly asked;

'Where is my brother?"

Morcar pointed to Cearl and with a jerk of his head ordered him to bring Tostig to the meeting. "Your brother is alive and well, Lord." He said cautiously.

"We shall see." Harold replied barely able to contain his fury. To Osfrid it appeared as though the man's anger was not aimed directly at Morcar but also at Tostig. A fact he found very interesting indeed.

After a few moments Cearl returned, accompanied by two Huscarl's escorting Tostig. Both of the grim faced warriors had their war axes in their hands ready to strike down their captive if anything at the meeting were to go awry. Tostig's weasel expression broke into a smile as he saw his brother.

"Harold my brother, how nice to see you." He said with sarcastic venom.

Harold stepped forward and embraced his brother awkwardly. Osfrid scowled as the realisation that Harold had no love for his brother hit home.

"You are well? Unharmed?" Harold asked.

"As well as can be expected brother." Tostig replied coolly.

Harold simply nodded in response before he turned his attention to Morcar and the Thegn's.

"I have a message from the King." He shouted to the crowd so that both noble and commoner alike would have no chance of misunderstanding or not of hearing him.

"You are to lay down your arms forthwith and to submit your grievances to a full assembly of the realm. If, you refuse to do this, then the King will consider you all outlaws, and condemn you to death." Harold looked at each of the Thegn's in turn as he spoke. His gaze was intense and some could not bear to see it and looked away.

Osfrid simply looked back. He didn't agree with Morcar's methods but the chance of ridding himself of Tostig's tyranny had to be made.

After Harold spoke, another tense silence fell over the watching crowd. His words sank into their minds and the realisation of how serious things had become hit home to many.

Edwin whispered to his brother for a few moments before stepping forward. He opened his arms wide as though bringing in all of the men watching towards him.

"You tell the King, that we Thegn's of the North acted as anyone would in the face of persecution and tyranny. Tell him, we will only lay down our arms if Tostig is exiled henceforth from the kingdom, his titles stripped and his lands dispersed to his victims. That my brother Morcar be officially made Earl of Northumbria in his place" A great cheer erupted from the on-looking warriors as they heard their demands being spoken. The cheering went on for several moments before Morcar urged the men to silence.

Tostig laughed. "You bastards think that the king and my brother will just give into your demands."

"Silence brother." Harold snapped. "You have caused enough trouble here. If I could, I would have you whipped for causing all of this." He turned to face Morcar and the others.

"Very well." He conceded. 'I will bring your demands before the King. I do not desire civil war, this kingdom cannot afford it." He gestured to his Huscarl's and his horse was brought to him. He hauled himself nimbly into the saddle as his bodyguard did the same. He turned his horse and trotted over to Morcar. "The King has summoned an assembly to be held in a week's time at Oxford. Come and let us avoid an unnecessary war."

Tostig sputtered at his brothers words. "These men should all die! Bring the army and kill them all"

Harold simply glared at him with a look of iron.

With that Harold and his bodyguards turned their mounts and galloped out of the camp in a clatter of hooves.

"You bastard!" screamed Tostig at his brothers retreating back

Osfrid stepped up behind him drawing his sword and putting its point to the back of his nemesis's neck. "You're not worth the lives that would be lost in a war to decide your fate." He growled into his sworn enemy's ear.

"The one who betrayed me. A clever man you are. How's your wife. I wonder if she still lives." Tostig growled back menacingly.

His words were like a fist and Osfrid stepped back in horror.

"What have you done?" Osfrid demanded fearfully. His heart sank. Cearl walked over to them and ordered one of the Huscarl's to restrain Tostig.

"Cearl too, you really thought that you could betray me and get away with it? Your families are all going to die for your acts of defiance. Even as we speak my men will be paying each of your homes a visit.

They too will know what it feels like to be stabbed in the back. Except in their case it will be actually happening." Tostig replied as he started to laugh manically.

Cearl halted and the colour drained from his face. Osfrid roared in frustration as he punched Tostig in the stomach. Tostig fell to his knees winded but still the laughs emanated from the wretch. Osfrid brought his sword up, preparing to put an end to the vile man before him once and for all, but before his blade fell onto Tostig's exposed neck it was knocked aside by Cearl's own blade.

"No, Osfrid no. We need the bastard alive. If he dies then the kingdom will surely go to war and we won't know what he has done to our families." Cearl shouted despairingly.

Osfrid glared at Cearl, the rage within him was almost impossible to control. He yelled in frustration and threw his sword away in anger.

"I cannot lose my family Cearl, not to him. I have to go, I have to protect them."

Cearl put an arm on Osfrid's shoulder. "That man is a liar; he may just be saying these things to weaken our resolve. Morcar needs us with him to convince the king to give in to our demands. And if he does speak the truth, we must have faith in those around our families to protect them."

*

The pitch black of the moonless night, hid the group of armed men moving stealthily through the long grass towards the camp. The orange glow created by dozens of slowly dying campfires backlit the area showing the sleeping figures of men. The majority of the army slept outside, only the Thegn's had their own animal hide tents to protect themselves from the bitter cold.

The leader of the group made a low whistle in the imitation of an owl call. Immediately the others halted and lay down onto their stomachs. The bitter biting cold of the rapidly approaching winter had already taken hold of the country causing the ground to be covered in a thick frost. Blades of grass that had been lush and soft in the summer months were now replaced by the hardness of ice.

A patrolling sentry walked close by to the leaders hiding spot. His armoured boots crunching noisily as he went.

Once the guard had passed the men began to move again, keeping low and staying out of the dim light being cast by the numerous campfires and torches.

The group had been following Morcar's army since the sacking of York.

They moved quickly and quietly with purpose towards the centre of the camp, being careful not to disturb any of the sleeping soldiers as they went. Many of the men slept close to the fires or wrapped up in whatever furs or whores they could find to keep out the biting cold.

Eventually the group reached the heart of the camp undetected. The tent that held their objective stood in the centre of a small clearing with a small campfire burning brightly in front of it. Two grim looking Huscarl's stood at either side of the tents entrance their large war axes in their grasp. Each wore thick coats of furs over their armour and wore thick fox hide hats. Both of them looked thoroughly annoyed at being assigned guard duty on such a bitingly cold night.

The group's leader gestured to two of his men to flank the tent and silently they edged their way around the clearing.

Other tents were scattered all around containing the sleeping forms of the rebel nobles and Thegn's. For a moment the leader considered if it would be worth killing as many as they could whilst they slept. He shook his head in frustration, his orders were clear. No unnecessary casualties.

A low whistle came from across the clearing; he looked up and spotted his two men in position at the tents flanks. The Huscarl's must have been drowsy for it surprised the leader that they didn't respond to the out of place noise. He'd give the fools a clip around the ear for their eagerness.

He dreaded to think what the outcome would be if the guards had been more alert.

Once more the leader made his bird call giving his men the signal to take out the two guards. Each of his men was equipped with a heavy club and a short sword called a Sax. In the heat of battle and within the condensed bodies of the shield wall the shorter blade was the best weapon to use when stabbing at your enemies.

His men slowly crept forward behind the Huscarl's and raised their clubs high. Simultaneously both men swung cracking the guards over the head with an audible thud. Both guards crumbled to the ground in a noisy crash. The leader and his men tensed waiting for an alarm to be raised, but as moments passed they breathed a sigh of relief as none was raised.

The leader stood and walked towards the tent, now that the guards were dealt with and no alarm had been raised getting back out again wouldn't be too difficult. He opened the cloth flap and smiled.

"My lord Tostig, We are here to rescue you."

Tostig awoke groggily and upon seeing his loyal servant he smiled wickedly.

***

9.

October 1065

Britford, Salisbury

Edwards's fury was unquenchable. For days he had stormed through the royal palace berating his servants and making the lives of his courtiers a misery. The King ranted and raved about disloyalty amongst his nobles, blaming everyone and everything but himself for the events unfolding in the North.

It was common knowledge that the nobles of the kingdom had little respect for the king, partly because he had allowed things to spiral out of control but mostly because of the Norman influence he had brought to the realm.

Edward had spent much of his youth in Normandy and made it clear that he preferred the Norman way of life than the customs and ways of his own subjects. The kings behaviour had become increasingly erratic, a fact that troubled Harold greatly.

It had been his own father the earl Godwin that had exiled Edwards beloved Norman courtiers after the Saxon nobles threatened to usurp him from the throne. Conflict had always been a way of life in the kingdom but Edward appeared to have little grasp of the events unfolding around him.

Harold watched the young serving girl flinch in fear as the king screamed in outrage at her. No doubt she had made some minor petty mistake that had set him off. She wept softly as the tirade continued. Finally Harold had enough of having to listen to his sovereigns grating voice and with a knock on the oak door entered the chamber.

Edward stopped his yelling and spun around to face whoever dared disturb him in mid flow. Upon seeing Harold he stood there trembling at him. Harold looked at the servant and waved her out of the room.

"Be gone girl." He said as he stepped aside to let her run past. Her sobs could be heard all the way down the long corridor.

A violent coughing fit struck Edward, almost causing him to collapse onto the reed covered floor.

Harold simply watched. He knew he should help his king, take his arm and lead him to the high backed oak chair in the corner of the room, but a wave of resentment slowed him.

A deep frustration ate at Harold's heart. It was obvious to him that Edward was toying with him. Why had he not declared Harold as his heir, to take the crown when he died? An event that Harold secretly hoped would be sooner rather than later. For Years he had run the affairs of the kingdom for the incompetent man before him, and still Edward was playing with him.

No, not just him, but other powerful men.

Rumours had reached him of the king sending messages to William of Normandy and word came from across the sea that Harold Hardrada, the powerful Viking king of Norway was casting an envious glance towards England.

Harold put an arm around the retching king and walked him slowly towards the chair.

"How dare they make demands of me?" Edward growled as Harold settled him into the chair. The King looked paler than usual after his latest bout of illness. The journey from London had taken a lot out of him and his coughing fits struck him more and more.

Harold stepped back and turned to face the open fire place. He threw a fresh log onto the embers and brought the flame back to life in a flurry of sparks and crackling timbers. The winter wasn't as severe in Britford as it had been on the journey South from Northampton. The first snows had started to fall as he made his way to the king's residence at the edge of the town.

The residence was an Old Saxon hall once used by the old kings during the Viking invasions. Its high oak beams and large open fireplaces kept the interior cosily warm. Edward had summoned his council here to discuss the northern rebellion; Harold knew the king lusted for blood and a military solution to the problem. A solution he was desperate to avoid.

"The Northern Nobles are angry my lord. My brother has been acting like a petty tyrant for too long." Harold replied as he stared into the flickering flames. He adjusted his long green cloak and wrapped it tighter around his shoulders.

Edward sneered at the response. "Tostig, Your brother has always been loyal to me and the crown. I favour him above all other nobles because of his honesty and love. These rebels will feel my vengeance and Tostig will be at the forefront, spilling their traitorous guts."

Harold turned to face the king a frown of worry etched onto his face. The king truly wanted war, an act that would weaken the kingdom and lessen his chance of seizing power when the fool died.

"How will Tostig lead when he is the rebel's prisoner?" Harold asked, intrigued at the kings rant.

A look of malicious glee crossed Edwards's features as he leaned back in his chair.

"My men freed your brother last night Earl Godwinson. You'll be pleased to know that he is making his way here to face my judgement. A judgment that I assure you will be favourable to a trusted servant of mine."

Harold stared at the king in shock. Edward had gone behind his back to rescue his idiot of a brother and now the situation would surely be made worse.

He could barely contain his outrage but swallowed his pride deeply and instead thanked the king for 'saving' his brother. He thought desperately. He would need the rebels on his side if he was to be made king when Edward died, but now thanks to the king's actions it would be difficult to win their trust. Now that they'd lost their main bargaining chip the rebels would become desperate.

War was inevitable.

He strode through the hall towards his own quarters deep in thought. Somehow he would have to salvage the situation. He would have to choose, either his brother or his ambitions for the crown and that was a choice he could easily make.

***

Northampton

The Earls gathered in Morcar's tent and their anger was palpable. Many demanded action that they should march south and onto London itself. Osfrid stood silently at the back of the group his thoughts fixed on his family and Tostig's mocking threats.

Now his enemy was once more free, snatched from underneath his very nose. He looked up to see Morcar animatedly talking to his brother and Cearl. For an hour they had discussed what they should do now that Tostig had escaped. No one seemed to have any idea about what should be done until finally Osfrid had had enough of the pointless debating. He pushed his way to the front of the Earls and slammed his fist down onto Morcar's writing desk. The loud sound caused Edwin to jump with a curse and silenced the bickering group.

"There is nothing to discuss."

He started loudly.

"Tostig may have escaped us but it does not change anything. He will ride to the King and beg his forgiveness, which Edward will surely grant."

"Then we will be hunted men. Tostig's vengeance will be brutal." one of the nobles shouted.

Osfrid nodded in agreement causing the group to start talking and arguing once more. He sighed heavily and once more slammed the desk forcing silence to descend once more.

"You all forget my lords, that it is neither Tostig nor Edward who wields the true power of this kingdom. Harold is the one we must win over. He has the loyalty of the southern nobles and I saw when they met that he has no love for his brother. He wants to be king and only our backing will allow him to do so."

Edwin laughed and clapped Osfrid on the shoulder.

"You speak well my friend. But tell me, why we should back Harold. He is not Edwards's heir. Anyone of us here in this tent has just as good a claim as he."

Osfrid paused to think before he replied, all eyes were upon him and the future of Morcar's rebellion and the fate of the kingdom rested on what he was about to say. He looked at every one of the men before him and caught their eyes. His gaze lingered on Cearl which the man replied with a nod of his head.

"We back Harold because we would all, I am sure rather die than see a Norman or a devil farted Viking be our king. We must stand together for the future, not just what will happen to us but the future of England rests upon what we do here today."

It took only a moment for his words to sink in before each of the nobles yelled out in agreement. They would all die before England was ruled by a foreigner ever again.

After the noise died down Morcar stood forward and gripped Osfrid by the wrist.

"It seems we are all in agreement. We will contact Harold and discuss terms with him. Tostig will be exiled I swear it. We will have peace."

The next morning Osfrid and Cearl were summoned to Morcar's tent. As usual the night had been bitterly cold and snow had fallen onto the encampment. The biting chill ate through the men's clothes and spirits. Osfrid wore a thick wolf fur coat over the top of his chainmail and leather bodkin.

His boots had taken all night to dry out next to the campfire outside of his tent and it annoyed him that just by walking through the grass they would become sodden again shortly. He passed by a group of spearmen who were practising forming a shield wall and he hoped that those men wouldn't be needed to form one against their king. Other men huddled about the campfires or drank flagons of mead to keep the chill at bay.

His footsteps crunched over the rock hard ground as he reached the tent. Nervously he fingered his sword. The dragon hilt was polished to magnificence and he had greased and waxed the blade himself the evening before. The frost and ice hampered the drawing of the vicious steel blade from the scabbard a reason why he now noticed many of the Huscarl's had disposed of theirs and now wore the blades naked on their hips.

His father Hunweld had trained him since he was a small boy the skills of a warrior. He made sure he was skilled with the sword, axe and spear. His father always said it was better to be able to fight with anything as you never know when your trusty sword may be broken in battle. Most Huscarl's preferred to fight using large two handed axes than swords. Each Housecarl was deadly with the fearsome weapons and was capable of cleaving a man in two with one mighty blow.

The dragon sword belonged to the old man and had been his most prized possession before he had departed for the East and the Golden city.

Osfrid always called his father the old man but really Hunweld was in his early forties and still bore a fearsome reputation. In Britain he was famous for campaigning with Earl Godwin against the Scots and Welsh and in the East if his letters were indeed true he was now the captain of a Varangian guard unit.

A twang of loneliness struck him as he thought of his father. The old man had devoted his life to raising his son after his wife died and Osfrid could not have wished for a better father, an aim he hoped his own children felt. Hunweld was infinitely kind but could at the same time be ruthless. If you were his friend he would die for you but if you were his enemy than god help them.

Osfrid hoped he was still alive, the last letter he had received was from over a year previously and the words had been troubling. The Normans were threatening the Byzantine presence in Italy and war was inevitable. The pope was backing the Norman armies that were pillaging their way throughout Europe and was using them as the papacies sword.

His thoughts were interrupted by the arrival of Cearl who wore similar garb to himself.

"Shall we?" said Cearl as he opened the tents flap and waved Osfrid in. Osfrid nodded curtly in thanks for the courtesy.

Morcar stood to meet them and wasted no time getting to the business at hand.

"My friends, He started "I have thought over what Thegn Osfrid said last night and I agree with him. Harold is the key to resolving this situation and getting what we want. Therefore I'm sending the two of you South to meet with him."

Morcar took a sealed scroll from his tunic and handed it to Cearl. "In this letter are our demands and what we will offer Harold. I sent a messenger last night after our meeting and fortunately he was able to get word to some of the earls men. He will meet with you in Amesbury at the tavern on the northern gate."

Later that day the two men rode hard for the stone walled town of Amesbury. Neither man wore their armour and carried no weapons except for their swords. They needed to enter the town unnoticed and to not draw attention to themselves, the rebels plan rested on the meeting that was to take place. Each carried a cloth sack that contained the food needed for the two day ride.

On the first day of the journey they made good progress as the cold weather eased the further south they went. In the evening they reached the wealthy town of Oxford and with what little gold they had they used to stay the night at a tavern. Osfrid had never been to the town before and was amazed by the beauty of its churches and high stone buildings. He had never been so far away from his home and lands in Yorkshire. Cearl laughed at his friend's fascination, the sights were not new to him as he had made the journey south many times in the past.

The next day they set out at the crack of dawn down the old decaying stone flagged roman road. A sudden rain shower soaked them both as the evening neared and with sighs of relief they arrived at Amesbury's earthen walls just after nightfall. They passed by the sentries with no problems and paid a small boy to take their horses to the nearby stables.

The town was the epitome of Saxon culture, taverns, churches and smithies lined the main street which was full of the townspeople busily going about their business. It wasn't hard for them to find the tavern that Harold had arranged to meet as it was the noisiest in the area. A group of drunkards staggered out into the street singing an old ballad horribly out of key.

A man was retching into the gutter whilst down a side alley people pissed and shitted the mead they had drunk. Cearl threw Osfrid an amused look before tightening his sword belt and entering.

Osfrid led the way and opened the wooden door that led into a large smoked filled room. A huge fireplace dominated the far wall that gave out more smoke than it did heat. The place was packed with patrons drinking and laughing. Groups of men and women sat around tables where the barmaids were constantly being groped by hungry bearded men.

"We need to find Harold." Said Cearl loudly, he had to raise his voice over the din. Osfrid nodded in agreement and made his way to the bar.

The stench of spilt mead and ale was overwhelming. After pushing their way through the packed room and reaching the bar, Osfrid grabbed one of the flustered looking barmen by the shoulder. The short balding man jumped in alarm at being touched but Osfrid calmed him by pulling a gold coin out from under his cloak.

"We're looking for someone and we are expected." He said shouting over the noise. A roar of laughter burst from a corner and the sound of shattering pottery made the bar man wince.

"Well sirs, as you can see it's very busy." The barman said eyeing up the gold coin greedily. "But I'm sure we can find who you're looking for."

The short man waved for them to follow as he made his way through the crowd. They reached a worn looking stair case that led up to the taverns second floor and the barman pointed for them to head up. Osfrid flicked the coin at the man in thanks and he and Cearl ascended the staircase.

They found themselves on a small landing which walls were covered in the heads of animals. A great stag hung from the highest wall and a wolf's from another. A narrow corridor with a half dozen doorways was up another small set of steps.

Giggles from the taverns whores and the grunts of their customers echoed down the hall and Cearl smirked as he thought about the irony of meeting a potential future king in such a place.

They made their way down the corridor and saw a man dressed in a long green cloak standing outside the far right-hand room. He glanced at them and banged once on the door. It swung open and the guard stood aside as he waved them inside the room and there they found Harold.

He was sat on a wooden stool with his hands held up to the small fire that was ablaze in the room's hearth. A large cloth covered window dominated the far wall and a lice infested bed and a bucket were the only other objects within. Harold was wearing a hooded cloak which he now removed.

"Greetings." He said gravely. "I trust your journey was a pleasant one."

"Pleasant enough, lord." Cearl answered politely.

Harold stood and poured himself a cup of water once more before sitting down onto his stool.

"Lets get down to business shall we? But wait where are my manners I don't even know your names."

"I am Thegn Osfrid Hunweldsen and this is Thegn Cearl of Acomb. We speak on behalf of Morcar and the lords of the North." Osfrid answered as he sat down heavily onto the bed.

“Hunweldsen? I remember hearing tales of your father and uncle. Very well then Thegn Osfrid, what does Morcar want?” Harold asked eagerly.

“Peace my Lord and justice.” Replied Osfrid earnestly.

“Noble aims, both of which I want as well. However, it is not I who makes these decisions.’ He opened his arms apologetically. ‘The king does, and I fear the King is beyond reasoning with. To put it bluntly my lords, he wants all of you to hang.”

“But surely you can change his mind.” Cearl asked nervously.

“Alas I fear my wretched brother will poison the king’s mind against me. He already believes that I betrayed him.” Harold said as he leaned forward putting his arms onto his knees. “At the royal council Tostig openly accused me of aiding you. Luckily my supporters turned the argument back against him, but it was very difficult to calm the king’s rage.”

“Then Tostig needs to be removed.” Osfrid growled.

“Be careful Thegn Osfrid. Tostig is still my brother;’ warned Harold darkly,

‘There is one way we can avoid war but I must have Morcar’s oath that he will support me.”

"At this point lord I believe Morcar will agree to anything to see his aims realised." Osfrid said cautiously.

"There is to be a meeting of the Witan in three days in Oxford. There the lords of the kingdom will gather to decide the next course of action. Even the king cannot overrule the decisions made there."

"I will use my influence to persuade the Southern nobles to refrain from war. A risky move for me as the king will be furious, and I will grant your demands."

"What will you want from us in return?" Cearl asked as he paced the room.

"To put it simply, I want the Northern nobles to back me to become king upon Edwards's death."

The request was no surprise to either of the Thegn's.

"What about your brother?" Osfrid demanded.

"He has become a liability to my aims. I will back you in your demand that he be exiled. However I will not allow any of you to kill him. If he dies before he is exiled then the deal is off. On my father's grave I swear it."

***

10.

Northumbria- near the Scottish border

Acca ducked as the woad wearing warrior swung his axe. The blue war paint gave the Scot a fearsome appearance.

Quickly he launched himself at the bigger mans chest and using his whole body weight he sent the Scot crashing to the ground. Acca used all of his strength as he desperately tried to prise the axe from his enemies grip. The Scot clawed at his face with his free hand trying to flip his prey onto his back. Acca never gave him the chance. He raised his right hand and balled it into a fist which he brought smashing down into the Scots face. With a satisfying snap the warrior's nose disintegrated upon impact and the man fell still.

Acca breathed a deep sigh of relief and rubbed the sweat from his brow. All around him were the screams of the border village's inhabitants.

It was dark and like demonic wraiths the Scottish raiders had emerged from the bleak countryside. He had been asleep in a stable as the first flaming torches struck the village. Wood and thatch ignited, casting a ghastly orange hue over the scene. Then the screams started.

Quickly he grabbed his sword and clothes, and ran to find Ceadda, but in the confusion he had lost his companion. It was then, as he stood in dumbfounded confusion that the semi naked warrior had attacked from the shadows. Acca spat derisively onto the unconscious form before running further into the village.

For four days he and Ceadda had been tracking the men who had taken Osfrid's family. A series of clues left by one of them was the only way they could keep on the right path. A silver brooch had been left one night, a scrap of cloth from a fine dress the next. The Fyrd had helped in the pursuit for the first day and night but as the distance from Driffield grew they were forced to return to their homes.

A hundred armed men would not go undetected through the wild and lawless lands of the far North of England. Ceadda had reluctantly sent them home to their wives' and children, but he himself had vowed to find his lords family no matter where it took him.

At first they had believed that the abductors were heading north and taking the family to Scotland but now they were certain they had changed direction and were headed east towards the sea. For what purpose he dreaded to think.

He rounded the corner of a house and saw that a group of village guards had grabbed weapons and had formed a motley shield wall in the village square. He squinted and saw that it was Ceadda who was leading them.

The big man was wearing his armour and swinging his war axe at the enemy. One Scot hurled a spear but it was easily blocked by a villagers shield. The group of defenders huddled tighter together as a dozen crazed warriors charged their lines. Ceadda's axe swung again, cutting down one of the attackers whilst the rest died on the tips of the villager's spears.

A shout came from the surrounding countryside and dozens of raiding Scots charged into the village. Ceadda bellowed orders to the panicked villagers and held the motley group of spearmen he had formed together.

Once more the shield wall tightened together, each mans round shield overlapping his neighbours and protecting them. However, this time the Scots had learnt, and were now hastily forming their own shield wall.

Acca ran towards Ceadda and quickly grabbed a spear that a cowering woman held out to him. He shouted his thanks before taking her arm and pushing her towards the small stone chapel where the women and children were rushing to for safety.

"Here lad, you'll need a shield." Ceadda said, surprisingly jovially as he noticed his young comrade had joined the defenders. He reached down and picked up a battered shield still in the grip of the poor man who had been holding it moments before.

"He didn't duck fast enough." Ceadda stated simply as Acca hefted the weight.

The Scots had finished forming their wall and were slowly advancing down the muddy street towards them. They chanted repeatedly as they approached unnerving some of the villagers. These men were farmers not warriors. Acca looked around him at the other defenders. Most were young men around his age, but others were boys barely able to keep their shields aloft.

"When they get close, stab at the bastards feet. Force their wall to break and we will survive this night." Ceadda called over the chants.

Sweat was pouring into Acca's eyes despite the freezing temperatures of the North. His heart raced and his palms were clammy. He'd only stood in a shield wall once before and that had been in York on that fateful day where he had made a promise, A promise that he might not have a chance to fulfil if he didn't last the night.

It felt like an eternity for the enemy to reach them, but when they did it was with a savagery that surprised him. The shields smashed against each other and it became a pushing match. In the shield wall there was no room to manoeuvre. Men from both sides shouted and screamed their fear and anger at their foes, Acca amongst them.

The deadlock broke within a few minutes as Ceadda once more raised his mighty axe and began to batter the Scots walls. With a powerful downward thrust the axe smashed an enemy shield to splinters taking the arm of the Scot holding it. Blood sprayed Acca's face but he didn't hesitate as the weakness exposed itself.

He thrust and stabbed with the spear impaling another enemy. All around him holes were beginning to open in the shield walls as men from both sides began to be cut down.

Only Ceadda's bellowed shouts of encouragement and threats kept the villagers from running and damning their families and homes to their savage attackers. Acca's spear lodged itself into the guts of a blue faced Scot; his foul breath filled his nostrils and spat up blood splattered into his face. He grunted as he released his grip on the spears shaft and kicked the dying man out of his way. The crush of the wall threatened to push him onto the spear points of the Scots who were slowly being pushed back.

Once more Ceadda smashed his way past the enemy's shields and with one crazed movement his axe dismembered three Scots in one brutal blow. Acca stepped back and drew the battered sword he had been given in Driffield. He cried a prayer to god to protect him before charging into the fray once more.

H e parried a spear thrust aimed at his head and lunged with the sword. The blade plunged deep into an enemies groin dropping him to the ground. The villagers pushed again and Ceadda battered down the Scots shields with his axe. More men fell but this time it was the Scots who looked panicked. They had come to the village for easy pickings and instead they had come up against a famed warrior and a determined bunch of defenders.

A horn sounded from out of the darkness. The raiders stopped and fled back into the darkness of the night, whooping and yelling as they carried away their booty. The moans of the dying and the victorious cheers of joy from the villagers reverberated throughout the cold night air.

Acca slumped onto the blood stained ground in exhaustion. Ceadda was being cheered by the villagers and those who had taken refuge inside the chapel re-emerged. The fires started by the raid were quickly extinguished and the people were glad to be alive.

"You did well Acca. I'll make a warrior out of you yet." Ceadda said proudly as he offered his hand to the younger man. Acca smiled tiredly and took the offered hand and stood up with a slight stagger.

"You hurt?" asked Ceadda.

Acca waved him away. "No just a few bruises." He winced as he tenderly touched his ribs.

"I need a drink." He stated with a smirk.

Ceadda laughed and led his young companion to a group of villagers. The men who had survived the shield wall were bringing out barrels of ale to celebrate their survival whilst the village's women were torturing the wounded and dying Scots. One had a dagger and was taking pleasure at slicing into the wounded mans flesh. His screams echoed through the night causing many of the men to cross themselves.

"They live in constant fear of rape and of being made widows because of those bastards. Who are we to judge?" Ceadda said as he noticed Acca's appalled expression.

*

The next morning Acca awoke with a pounding headache. He'd drunken himself to oblivion to forget the horror of the night before. He moaned in pain as his head ached and the bruises he'd sustained during the fight began to turn into vicious looking blues and purples. He opened his eyes and found himself on a bed of straw inside a barn.

A naked woman lay next to him her breasts exposed to the chill air. After the victory the village's girls had been more than willing to repay the strangers that had saved them. He didn't remember much but images of the buxom brunette next to him flashed into his mind. He smiled. He was finally a man albeit he couldn't really remember the act. He found his clothes scattered amongst the straw and dressed himself. He'd wasted too much time already. The sun was approaching its highest point of the day which meant the abductors of Osfrid's family had increased their lead on them.

He wrapped himself against the cold and half staggered and half walked to the village centre where he found Ceadda passed out in the chapel's small cemetery. Vomit was in his beard and only his loud snoring indicated that he was still alive. On his lap was his trusty war axe which he held in a loose grip.

Acca shooed off a gaggle of small children who had gathered around their drunken hero.

Acca went to the village well and filled up a bucket with the ice cold water. With a chuckle he emptied its contents onto his friends head. Ceadda lurched awake with a bellow and after a few moments of thrashing about like a wallowing pig he burst out laughing.

"Come on you old fool we've got to get a move on." Acca said in-between his chuckles. Ceadda looked at him bleary eyed and shook his head. He looked like a dog shaking itself dry after a swim.

"There's no need to hurry lad. I know just where the bastards are going." He said blurrily.

" And just how do you know that?" Acca said surprised.

"I spoke with the village chief. He said that the only place within a day's ride east is a place they call the Vikings cove."

"That doesn't sound good." Acca frowned in worry.

Cearl dragged himself up onto his feet and staggered off down the village's street. "There's no time to waste." He slurred.

"I thought you just said there was no rush!"

Acca rolled his eyes. "I'll get the horses. You need to sober up." He chuckled.

***

11.

October 1065

Oxford

The council of the Witan gathered in the great hall, the summons for the gathering had been dispatched several days previously and now the kingdoms lords and Thegn's entered the old town in ever increasing numbers.

Osfrid and Cearl had waited in the town after their meeting with Harold and had dispatched a messenger with the agreed terms to Morcar's camp. Word quickly spread throughout the realm that the rebel army had been spotted on the road north and that they had halted and set up a fortified base on a grassy plain a day's ride from the town.

A nervous tension had fallen on the populace, the kings troops had taken to patrolling the streets and Harold's Huscarl's were positioned on the walls. It was common knowledge that the king was itching for a fight and it was said that only Harold's refusal to field his army had prevented a battle.

"Look." Cearl said, pointing out a small group of horsemen approaching the town's gate.

The two Thegn's had been walking the walls and speaking with some of the Southern nobles. It appeared that Harold would get his wish of avoiding battle.

Osfrid squinted and shielded his eyes from the dazzlingly bright sun that shone high in the cold frigid sky. Sure enough he could make out the rapidly approaching figures of Morcar and his brother Edwin. Each wore their best armour, mail coats polished to a dazzlingly bright sheen covered by long cloaks. Morcar's black and Edwin's a rarely seen purple.

"It seems like things are going to be finally settled." Cearl muttered.

"Not settled enough for my liking." Osfrid growled in response.

He had returned to Harold the previous night and had argued that Tostig should be given over to the rebels. Osfrid pleaded that he needed to know what he had meant by the threats to his and Cearl's families, and as he had expected his plea had been rejected.

The two Thegn's watched as the town's gate was opened by a group of spearmen.

Osfrid saw that Morcar entered the town with his head held high like some conquering hero, with his brother mimicking the affect. Edwin had always been an arrogant man but now that he had finally manoeuvred himself into a position of real power that arrogance was threatening to overwhelm the man that Osfrid had once been good friends with.

At midday the town's church bells began to toll signalling the beginning of the great Witan. Earls and nobles made their way through the streets towards the king's palace situated on a slight bluff overlooking the town square. The splendid stone church dominated the wooden houses and market stalls around it.

It took almost an hour for all of the nobles to finally crowd into the palaces meeting hall. Over a hundred men were packed into the spacious chamber. Morcar's supporters were on one side and Harold's on the other.

In the centre was a wooden high backed throne in which the king sat and standing next to him was Harold and the archbishop of York. Clergy men were invited to the meeting to record and write down what was to be said.

The Archbishop was called Ealdred, a middle aged man with a long greying beard and a tonsured haircut. He wore the ornately decorated white robes of a bishop and carried a long black crooked staff. He stepped forward and called the crowd to silence. The crowd went quiet and every man knelt before the King.

"My lords." he called. "By the power of God and by the order of his majesty I pronounce this Witan as begun."

Edward looked pale and sickly but sat with a burning fire in his eyes. He stared at Morcar and his supporters with fury. That gaze made Osfrid feel uneasy and the urge to grasp his sword hilt was overwhelming. His hand reached for the pommel but only found air. As was the law, everyone who attended witan or entered a lord's hall had to surrender their weapons.

A few minutes were spent introducing several priests and nobles before the true business began. Edward raised a gloved hand and gestured to the back of the room.

The oak doors at the back of the chamber opened and once again Osfrid wished he had a blade, for in the open doorway stood Tostig. A wretched smirk of defiance was on his face as he cockily strode through the crowd to stand before the King. He knelt before Edward and kissed the royal ring that adorned his gloved hand.

Osfrid frowned as he noticed Edward smile at his enemy. It was a smile of friendship and once more a knot of doubt wound its way into his gut. He glanced at Cearl and saw the same look of concern mirrored on his face and many of the other Thegn's that had rebelled that fateful day. He watched Harold closely and was relieved to see the same look of annoyance on his handsome features that he had seen at the camp in Northampton.

Edward gestured for Tostig to stand at his side before standing and addressing his nobles.

"I have summoned this Witan, to resolve an issue that threatens to tear my kingdom asunder." He turned to face Morcar and a look of utter contempt crossed his features. He waved him forward and ordered him to kneel.

"You, Morcar son of Ælfgar have led a rebellion against your Lord Tostig and have committed treason against the crown."

A roar of protest burst out of Morcar's supporters and a dozen Huscarl's had to step into the centre of the crowd to part them.

Morcar spat.

"You say I have committed treason!" he roared above the din. "But I say that Tostig Godwinson has committed treason, Treason against his own people!" A cheer and shouts of agreement filled the chamber, this time it was Tostig's supporters that shouted their angry protests. Osfrid added his voice to Morcar's and edged his way towards the front of the jeering crowd.

"Silence!" bellowed Harold and once more the Huscarl's parted the two groups. Anger simmered, the tension grew.

"We are here to find a peace. Can no peace be made?" he demanded as silence descended once more.

Edward gestured to Harold who leant in close to hear the whispers of his king. Tostig meanwhile stepped forward.

"You and your followers have brought death and chaos to the north, the lands I hold in keeping for his majesty. You have committed greater crimes than I Morcar. You attacked York killing dozens of loyal spearmen, you sacked

Northampton slaughtering its inhabitants and yet here you are defying your king, I say he wants the throne for himself." He said passionately.

Osfrid felt a pang of guilt and regret as those words were spoken. He himself had argued strongly against the brutal sacking of the town. He still heard the screams of those women and children as they were either raped or put to the sword.

"The sacking of Northampton was necessary. " Replied Morcar defiantly.

That statement was met with fierce derision by Tostig's followers.

"They were Tostig's supporters; we had no choice, we could ill afford to have an enemy force behind us as we marched south to have our voices heard by his majesty."

Edward stood up and pointed a quivering finger at the rebels. "I should have you all killed for your treason!" he yelled in barely controlled anger. "But, Earl Harold has urged me to caution." He scowled at Harold as he spoke.

Osfrid could see the fury in the king's features and for a moment felt a pang of fear. Harold however took his chance to throw in his support for the rebels. Now was the time for him to ensure his future.

"I see that there will be no reconciliation as long as both sides will not back down." He turned and looked harshly at his brother, who stared defiantly back.

"My brother is the cause of all this."

Edward tried to protest, the king hadn't seen Harold's game, and instead he had been blinded by his lust for vengeance and his love for Tostig. Harold spoke over the king's feeble voice.

"We cannot afford a civil war. A winter campaign in the north would be far too difficult and costly." Harold spoke at the king as though Edward was a simple child. "Therefore I propose an alternative solution to this matter." The hall fell into an expected silence. Osfrid held his breath, could it be that he was about to be finally free of his most hated enemy?

"Tostig shall be exiled from the kingdom forthwith, his lands and title are to be granted to Morcar, and in exchange the Northern Thegn's and nobles shall reaffirm their allegiance to you, your majesty."

For a moment all eyes fell onto the king. Then the whole room exploded with shouts of agreement to Harold's proposal. Osfrid bellowed loudly as did Cearl and Edwin. The nobles from the south added their agreement and the decision was made.

Edward had gone pale and a spasm could be seen under his left eye. He was visibly shaking with rage. His usually pale skin flushed with anger.

With a gesture from Harold two Huscarl's restrained Tostig causing a fight to break out between the two brother's supporters.

"Bastard!" Tostig screamed at his brother as he was dragged away. "I swear to god I will put an end to you and spill your traitorous guts, I will cut out your heart and hang it above my mantle."

His shouts faded as the doors were closed again.

Now the matter of Morcar's ascension to Earl would take place but Osfrid hadn't the stomach for that. He had never been interested in his power play; instead he slipped out of the hall and followed the Huscarl's dragging off Tostig.

"Wait." He called to the Huscarl's, "I have business with this man."

The two warriors recognized Osfrid and dropped Tostig to the floor in a dishevelled heap.

Osfrid knelt down and gripped his foe by his hair. "Now you will tell me what you meant." He growled into his ear.

Tostig recognised Osfrid's voice and spat onto the stone flagged floor. Even, as he was about to be exiled and betrayed by his own brother the man still showed a steely defiance.

"Osfrid. You should drop this obsession with your family, it makes you look pathetic." He replied sarcastically.

Rage flowed through Osfrid; all he wanted was to know that his family was safe. He shouted in frustration; "Just tell me!"

He smashed Tostig's face into the stone floor causing blood to pour from the bastard's nose. Tostig simply laughed. Osfrid shouted out again in frustration and again smashed his enemies face into the ground. He raised Tostig's head once more.

The guards looked on, unsure whether to stop him.

"Wait, wait. I will tell you." He sputtered. "I tell you this, because I want to see the look on your face as I reveal their fate."

"Just tell me God damn you!" Osfrid yelled as he stood up in frustration, his patience was running out fast and despair was threatening to engulf him.

"Your family were taken by my men Osfrid. I'd been watching you for some time you see. I knew you'd betray me at some point just like your friends did. So I gave the order to take them as hostages, to keep you docile and in my thrall. But alas along came Morcar and that plan was scuttled." He paused to spit a mouth full of blood at Osfrid's feet.

"The man I charged with taking your family is a wretch. He works with a Dane, a monster of a man." He chuckled.

Osfrid struck him rocking his head back and causing more blood to pour.

"Give me a name!"Osfrid roared.

"Handel, his name is Handel."

The name was familiar to Osfrid and as he remembered where he had heard it a new sense of dread clawed inside of him. Handel was rouge, a murderer a rapist and a slaver. He'd spent many months trying to hunt the beast down after he and a band of other outlaws had raided farmlands not far from Driffield. He knew of the slavers that raided the coastal areas of the north, they were mostly lord-less Vikings from Denmark or Norway, scum the lot of them.

He now knew what had happened to his family. A man like Handel would realise the worth of a noble's family and would either hold them to ransom or sell them for a large sum of gold to slavers. The man's greed gave him some comfort; there was still a chance they yet lived.

His thoughts were interrupted by Cearl who came striding down the corridor.

He glanced nervously at the Huscarl's then his gaze settled onto Tostig. "Morcar is now Earl of Northumbria, he has taken your lands and wealth and any man who will not swear an oath to him from your supporters will die." He stated off handily to Tostig.

He reached down and hauled Tostig back onto his feet. "What did you do with my family?" he asked threateningly.

"They're dead Cearl. I gave the order the day of the attack on York. You were one of my most vocal detractors what did you expect?" Tostig replied nonchalantly.

Devastation struck Cearl and a cry of utter misery echoed down the hall.

***

12.

North East Coast

Look," yelled Ceadda over the sound of galloping hooves. "Down there by the sea."

Acca squinted and could just make out the fearsome sight of a Viking Longboat riding low in the tide. The journey to the coast had taken two hours at full gallop, and relief had filled him as he picked up the relatively fresh trail of a group of travellers.

As they got closer they could see people moving hastily along the shoreline. Ceadda shouted in joy as he recognised the dishevelled figures of Osfrid's family being pushed toward the sea and the awaiting boat.

"We can't let them reach that boat, come on!" Acca shouted as he spurred his horse onwards. He willed the horse to move faster, the longboat was rapidly approaching the sandy shore.

"They've seen us." Ceadda said as he drew his battleaxe. Sure enough one of the figures they didn't recognise turned to face them, a deadly looking war spear held in his hands. The man was massive, built like a bear and sure to have a similar strength.

Desperation filled Acca's soul as he saw the longboat run aground and begin to unload a group of heavily armoured Norse warriors. They were now only a few hundred yards away and the screams of the two captured women could be heard on the wind.

He narrowed his eyes and focused on the big man with the spear. He deftly drew his sword and roared a challenge as his horse charged home.

The big man roared back, and with a speed that took Acca by complete surprise whirled his spear above his head and threw it with devastating power. It was a throw that any man would be in awe of. The deadly spear point glinted in the faint sunlight as it soared through the air and struck his horse killing the trusty steed outright and mid gallop. Acca screamed in terror as the horse lost its strength, and smashed into the sand head first, sending its rider flying through the air and crashing into the dunes.

Ceadda roared in anger at seeing his friend felled and slammed his horse into the big man sending him to the ground with a crunch. Ceadda jumped from the saddle and parried a sword blow aimed at his heart. The Viking warriors surged towards him causing him to fight with a desperate determination.

Aerlene whirled around as she saw the two riders charging her captors. Her eyes widened as she recognised her husband's trusted steward and a man she did not know, attacking the vermin that now pushed her children towards the waiting boat. Esma gripped her brother's hand tightly as the skirmish began and screamed when the handsome stranger's horse was felled by Gulbrandr. Their other captor, Handel drew his sword and lunged at Ceadda.

"My children run!" Aerlene screamed as she saw a chance to escape.

Just as she was about to flee, large rough hands grabbed her by her hair and threw her to the ground, "Where are you going bitch?" Handel cackled viciously. Esma screamed as she too was grabbed by one of the newly arrived Viking warriors. Wulf however was small and nimble; he slipped from the grasp of the warrior sent to restrain him and ran away as fast as his legs could take him.

*

Acca groaned as he sat up spitting sand from his mouth and shaking it from his hair. Quickly he saw Ceadda being held at bay by half a dozen fearsome looking Vikings in a shield wall, Osfrid's wife and daughter being dragged aboard the longboat and a small boy running away up the beach. He rolled to his feet and picked up his sword. He saw the large Dane that had killed his mount dragging himself back onto his feet, he gulped as the monster of a man set eyes upon him and a wicked grin crossed his features.

"Ceadda, we have to stop the boat" he called. The older man nodded and with a roar charged the wall. He swung his axe savagely and desperately trying to break the wall which was now retreating towards the boat. Acca could see that the wall would not break; Viking warriors were different to Scottish savages.

Despair filled him as he saw the two women being roughly dragged aboard, their screams tearing at his heart. His attention snapped back to the big man approaching him.

Blood poured from a cut on his head into his beard giving him a demonic appearance. In his hand he carried the now broken in half spear.

"Come on you bastard." Acca growled.

They began to move around each other, sword held high, spear held low. Acca feinted with a shift of his shoulder. The Dane read the feint and forced him back a step, with a lunge of the spear. The blades clashed and the fight began.

The Dane bellowed as he swung the spear point narrowly missing Acca's chest. Acca parried another blow and launched a series of quick thrusts and cuts, they struck coming together in a twist of sweat and straining muscle. Acca took two quick steps forward and brought his blade up in a neat slice, breaking the Danes defence and cutting deeply into the growling mans chest.

The Dane grunted in surprise as Acca pressed his attack without pause, slash after slash. Each was parried by shifts of weight and movements of the spear. Sweat poured into Acca's eyes. Desperation filled him as he tried to think of new moves to break his foes defences. He flailed and missed and, as he lost balance the Dane struck sinking the spear point into Acca's abdomen.

He cried out as he felt his strength give out. His legs seemed weak sticks and gave way under him. Blood splattered the sand, but the colours had gone from his sight replaced by the thump of his heartbeat and flashes in his eyes.

"Pathetic Saxon dog" the Dane spat as he stood over his defeated foe.

Just as he was about to deliver a killing blow Ceadda tackled the Dane to the ground, his fight with the sheildwall forgotten to save his young friend.

"Forgotten me?" He shouted at the Dane as they untangled from one another.

The two large men stood glaring at one another; one armed with an axe the other spear. For a heartbeat neither moved then suddenly and with explosive force the two fighters smashed into each other.

Ceadda began his attack, in past the Danes guard and out again before his opponent could react. He buried his axe deep into the Danes chest piercing both flesh and bone. Blood burst from the mortally wounded mans mouth before he crumpled into the sand, Blood pooling under the corpse. Ceadda hurried over to Acca he knelt down and raised him into a sitting position.

"The family..." Acca tried to say.

"They're gone." Ceadda replied miserably.

"The shield wall was too strong I couldn't get to them in time. The boat is already off the beach, seems we got here just as the tide came in."

Acca groaned in pain and misery. He had failed in his promise to the man who had saved his life.

"Rest here friend. It seems not all has been lost." Ceadda said as he pointed to a small boy hiding amongst the sand dunes.

It was Wulf, Osfrid's son.

Part Two

Quest

13.

January 1066

Westminster

Harold Godwinson strode through the corridors of the palace, a sense of nervous excitement coursing through his veins.

The King was on the verge of death, the last three months had taken everything out of the old man and now Harold's chance had arrived.

He stopped, and listened to the howling wind raging outside. The winter had struck with an ominous ferocity, heavy snow and terrible storms had ravaged the land.

Many priests were preaching that the end of days was coming, famine and disease was rife. He leaned against a pillar and looked out of a window.

The cold from outside blew in chilling him and forcing him to wrap his green woollen cloak tighter about himself. London lay calm and snow covered before him.

Thatched roofs lay as far as the eye could see, interspersed with church spires and rising smoke from countless hearths.

The populace was suffering but none more so than him. His conscious was troubling him.

The exile of his brother had weighed heavily on his heart. Once they had been close, had even fought and bled together against the realms enemies. Now he was his foe.

The King had loved Tostig, and had seen the earl's rebellion as a personal insult to himself and his Queen, a series of seizures had struck him in his grief at the loss of his friend and for weeks it had been Harold not Edward who had run the nation.

Morcar and the other Northern Earls had kept the peace, and in exchange Harold had repeatedly denied and thwarted Edward's demands for Tostig to be retried. Now finally as the winter struck in its full ferocity the king was in his death bed and the matter of succession was on everyone's mind.

In this matter Harold had no doubt who should take the crown.

It would be him and no other.

He was the best candidate by far. Edward's nephew was a weakling and would never gain the respect needed to keep the kingdom together and united.

He watched as a blackbird swooped down and landed in the courtyard below, its orange beak desperately seeking food buried under inches of snowfall. After a few minutes the bird was rewarded with its prize of a long fat juicy looking worm which it devoured greedily.

Harold shuddered at the sight, for him that was the fate he envisioned for England if he did not become King.

Its enemies would peck away at her soil until one emerged victorious and devoured her whole.

"Not as long as I draw breath." He uttered before turning away and returning to his quarters.

*

Driffield

"Will this bloody weather ever relent?" moaned Ceadda as he lost his footing for what must have been the fiftieth time that morning. The snow was waist high and the small boy that was accompanying him was almost buried completely. He gripped the boy and hauled him up onto his shoulders.

"At least you should stay dry little master." He said to Wulf.

The young boy smiled impishly.

They had headed into the village to buy a new axe head for the estate when they had been caught in yet another snow flurry. Both of them wore heavy animal fur cloaks over their woollen clothes, but the chill still seeped in.

"Will father be back soon?" Wulf asked sheepishly.

Whenever the boy spoke of his father these days he would look away in shame. Ceadda sympathised with the lad. Ever since they returned to Driffield the boy appeared to be wracked with guilt at having fled from his captors and, repeatedly Ceadda had tried to tell him none of it was his fault.

Osfrid had returned from Oxford a few days after the failed rescue on the beach and upon seeing his son run out to greet him Osfrid's eyes had widened with happiness.

He embraced his only son with a fierce love, joy on his face. But then he had called out to his wife and daughter. He saw the looks of sorrow on Ceadda's face and a devastating grief had overwhelmed him. The happiness Osfrid had felt had been torn away and the little boy had blamed himself.

Ceadda clamped his large hands onto the small boy's shoulders and knelt down to the lad's eye level.

"Aye lad he'll be back soon don't you worry. He said trying to reassure the boy. "You have to be strong for your father and strong for your mother and sister."

Tears threatened to spill from Wulf's eyes at the mention of his lost mother and sibling. Angrily he wiped them from his eyes and bit back the emotions.

"Are they even still alive Adda?" the boy asked miserably using the pet name he always called the gentle giant of a man who had helped raise him since he was a baby.

Ceadda squeezed the miserable boy's shoulders tightly. "You're Ma and sister still live boy, your father believes so, and if he does that's enough for me. He'll search the world and nay even hell itself to find them, and god help any man who gets in his way."

Wulf sniffed miserably and took Ceadda's hand as they continued their long walk back home.

It took them close to an hour before they crested the hill that overlooked the valley in which Osfrid's hall lay. The wooden palisades were blanketed in thick snow causing the place to merge with its surroundings. An unknowing traveller would have to look extra hard just to spot the structure, only the wisps of wood smoke gave an inkling to its presence.

The small stream than ran under the rise on which the hall and outhouses stood was frozen over, some children were playing on the banks and a hunter could be seen returning home with a handful of dead birds over his shoulder. The hunter yelled a greeting to Ceadda, who responded by waving an arm in recognition.

Since Osfrid's return the place had come back to life. The smithy was constantly busy preparing tools or forging new blades, the carpenters were constantly chopping wood and repairing the palisades and houses. The only thing missing however was happiness. The people of Driffield knew of their master's misery and the mood had infected them all.

Ceadda was shaken from his thoughts by the insistent tucking on his sleeve by Wulf. He glanced down at the boy.

"Adda, what's that banner flying over the hall?"

Ceadda frowned and was about to ask what banner, when he too saw it.

A white cross was emblazoned on a blue background and flapped proudly in the breeze.

"It can't be?" he muttered in wonder. "Who else could it be?"

Wulf looked at him in confusion and concern.

Ceadda laughed at the little boy.

"Don't worry lad. It looks like your grandfather has come."

*

Hunweld Hunweldsen stood in front of the hearth warming his large hands in the fierce flames heat.

The voyage back to England had been long and tortuous but the feeling of relief he had felt as he set foot back onto his homelands soil was indescribable.

Wulf sat on the reed strewn floor and looked at his grandfather in awe. In his early fifties, he had a bushy grey beard and despite his years a head of thick hair that reached to his shoulders which he wore in a single knotted ponytail. His shoulders were massive from years of swinging his beloved war axe *Rapture*. In height he was similar to his son and both men shared similar features. Both had fierce blue eyes, but Hunweld had a deep scar over his right eye socket caused by a Saracen blade.

"Where is my son?" he asked in a quiet but deep voice.

Ceadda stepped forward.

"He said that he was in the south gathering supplies for a voyage my lord. He should be back any day now." He said nervously, despite Ceadda only being a few years younger than Hunweld he was the only man to make him nervous. Ceadda had been Hunweld's brother in arms and had fought many battles against the Kingdoms enemies; it was the man's almost supernatural prowess that made men pause in awe and wonder. Ceadda went on to tell the tale of the loss of Osfrid's family and all that had transpired in the kingdom since the sacking of York.

"My daughter in law and my granddaughter are to be sold as slaves?" Hunweld said with venom in his voice. "That toad Tostig will pay."

"He will father." Boomed Osfrid's voice as he strode into the hall and embraced Hunweld.

"It is good to see you father." He said as he stepped back from the embrace and picked up Wulf from off of the floor causing the little boy to laugh.

Osfrid looked around his hall and frowned as he saw a dozen men he didn't recognise mooching around and helping themselves to mead and food.

"Friends of yours?" asked Osfrid with a raised eyebrow.

Hunweld laughed boomingly.

"Friends, aye you could say that lad. These fellows are the meanest sods you'll ever meet. These are my Varangian." He opened his arms wide and on hearing their name the men shouted in greeting.

Osfrid could see that the men were from many different places, he could see Norsemen, dark skinned Greeks and a handful of other nationalities.

Hunweld had served as captain in the Byzantine Empires Varangian guard for years and had made a fortune fighting for the empire. Norsemen, Russ, Bulgars and many other warriors travelled to the east to offer their services to the Emperors.

"Not one of the buggers speaks Anglisc sadly, this is the first time in five years I've been able to have a proper conversation." He cackled.

Osfrid put Wulf down and poured himself a cup of mead before turning back to face his father. A puzzled look was apparent on his face.

"If that's the case then how do you talk to them?" he asked.

"Latin or Greek.' Hunweld replied, "All those who serve the empire have to learn either one of those languages. I know both." He added proudly with a grin.

Osfrid had been taught Latin when he was a boy and now dug around in his memory for some words. He faced the fierce looking men and uttered a few phrases that serviced cloudily in his mind.

Wulf looked at his father in confusion as he said the strange words.

"What did you say papa?" he asked.

Osfrid frowned as the men laughed at his clumsy attempt.

"Hello I think." He muttered.

Hunweld bellowed with laughter and chided his son for his lack of learning.

"I forget how little an education is respected in this land.' He turned to Wulf and frowned. 'The boy needs an education Osfrid, is that scoundrel Elgar still alive?"

Elgar was a monk from York and had been a family friend for many years. He was a good teacher and had taught Osfrid how to read and write as a child. The old man was clever but had a reputation for chasing the ladies despite his religious background.

"Aye he still lives, last I heard he was at the monastery not far from here. But father we have more pressing matters to discuss than Wulf's education.' Pain entered his voice as he went on; 'My wife and daughter are captive somewhere across the sea, I've spent the past few weeks arranging a ship and supplies to go after them."

Hunweld put an arm over his son's shoulders.

"We will get them back. I promise you that."

***

14.

Acca waited patiently for the fisherman to finish putting away his nets and pots. Idly he watched the sea washing upon the shore, its rhythmic sound comforting, like a heartbeat of the Earth. His wounds were almost healed, only a livid scar remained on his abdomen where the spearhead had narrowly missed puncturing his stomach. For weeks he'd been forced to rest at Driffield unable to get the vision of the young woman he let slip away out of his mind. Her large blue eyes had penetrated into his soul. It had only been for a split second that their gazes had met but to Acca it felt like an eternity had passed.

The fisherman finished his task and gestured for Acca to follow. After a brief walk along the shore they arrived at a small shack which the fishermen used as a storehouse. The acrid smell of smoked fished wafted into his nose making his stomach growl in hunger. The winter so far had been extremely difficult for both the rich and poor. Supplies were running dangerously low across the land but these fishermen seemed to be doing well for themselves.

The elderly fisherman sat down on a wooden stool with a grunt of satisfaction as he looked over the days catch. Two huge earthen ware jars were crammed to the brim with all sorts of fish.

"I can tell ye what ye want to know." The old man said.

Acca's spirits rose and for the moment his hunger was forgotten. It had taken him days and many misleads to find this old man. Not many men on the Yorkshire shore knew the coast as intimately as the man he now sat with.

"The slavers come twice a year, once in the spring and again in the autumn. Some trips they come for nothing but other times I've heard the Scots tribes and vagrants of the wilds deliver a lot of unfortunates to them.' The man paused as he picked dirt from under his fingernails. 'They say a Norseman called Olaf Fork beard is the one behind them. Can get a lot of coin for Saxon slaves I hear."

Acca leaned in closer and asked; "Where does he come from? What port?"

The old man clucked his tongue against the roof of his mouth, deep in thought for a few moments.

"I heard he sails from a port in Norway. Oslo is the place."

"Have you ever been there?" enquired Acca.
The old man smiled revealing a set of yellow and black teeth.

"Aye I've been there. It was years ago, but I sailed there with a merchant vessel. The Norse don't take kindly to Saxons, we got ourselves into many a scrap I tell ye."

Acca thanked the old man and left the hut. Finally they had a place to start looking, Osfrid would be pleased.

Oslo, Norway

The smell of rotting fish and the deafening noise of a bustling market battered the senses of Esma and Aerlene. The voyage to this cursed place had taken more days then they cared to remember.

The rough winter seas had made them sick to their stomachs and it annoyed them that their captors seemed to have enjoyed the ordeal. Aerlene had heard tales of the Norsemen, of how they loved the sea and battle. As a little girl she had once seen a Norse raiding ship, her mother told her that she should thank god that those devils were no longer the scourge they once were.

She knew her husband had always been vigilant against their return, she remembered how he had spent an entire summer building watchtowers on the coast. Even Tostig had feared them. She almost laughed at the irony of it all. One nightmare had been replaced by another. She felt as though God had abandoned her.

They had spent the past month in a horrible little stone hut which was perched precariously close to the shoreline. Sleeping was difficult as the incessant sound of lapping waves and the bellows and calls of the seabirds and sailors kept them awake. The floor was caked in mud with a few reeds scattered above it, there was no fire and only a solitary candle provided them with light. High up on the south facing wall was a single barred window that looked out across the sea and to home.

"How long are they going to keep us here mother?" asked Esma. The young woman was covered in filth and her shift dress was torn after fighting off the advances of one the jailors. Aerlene sighed, she was doing her best to protect her daughter but knew the lusts of men, and it was only a matter of time, both for herself and her daughter.

"No doubt that bastard Handel will be bartering with the Norsemen, trying to get a good price for us." Esma spat. Aerlene frowned at her young daughter. She was a beauty but had a mouth as foul as a latrine.

Just as she was about to chastise her child the sound of keys jangling held her tongue. After a few moments a key clicked into the cell doors lock and with a squeak the thick pine door slowly opened.

Standing in the doorway was Handel, his rat like face sneering as usual. Standing behind him was a extremely tall and extremely fat Norseman.

His blonde hair fell to his barrel like chest and his eyes were a steely grey.

The man's beard was so long it almost touched the floor and would have if not for the two torques holding it in place. The shape was that of a forking road and Aerlene was mesmerised by it, she'd never seen a beard like it before.

The two men conversed briefly in Nordic before the fat man stepped into the cell and grabbed Aerlene pulling her close to towards him. Esma cried out but was silenced as Handel slapped her onto the ground.

"My name is Olaf Forkbeard." The Norseman said haltingly in Anglisc. "You are my property now." He leered at Aerlene as he ran his eyes greedily over her body.

With a sudden movement he ripped her already damaged and torn dress from off of her shoulders. She gasped and tried to cover her now exposed breasts. Olaf batted her hands away and grabbed at them forcefully causing her to scream out in pain.

"I like to try out my latest buys before I sell them on." He grinned. Aerlene spat in his face but was only rewarded with a pitiless laughter. Forcefully he grabbed her arm and dragged her out of the cell.

"MOTHER!" screamed Esma.

She lunged for her but was once more sent sprawling to the ground by Handel who was roaring with laughter.

The two men left the cell dragging Aerlene with them. Her pitiful cries could be heard as the heavy door slammed shut. They faded as she was taken further and further away.

Esma collapsed in tears. Surely she would share a similar fate.

Westminster Palace

The mournful tones of the cities church bells tolled out across the city summoning the people to vespers. To the occupants of the king's grand bedroom that call to prayer had been answered. The King lay in his bed pale and gaunt. One side of his face had dropped slightly as a result of the strokes that afflicted him. His hair had fallen out leaving only strands that clung feebly to the royal scalp beneath them. The room was thick with the smell of incense and smoke from the fireplace that roared at the far end of the chamber.

Edward wore a gold and red satin nightgown that only extenuated his decrepit appearance. Once a man, a king, which was feared he now lay like a feeble child waiting for his god to take him.

Harold Godwinson and his younger brother Gyrth stood at the back of the room away from the monks and bishops that crowded about the bed.

"The bugger had better announce an heir before he croaks it." Gyrth grumbled quietly. The younger Godwinson had never had much love for the King. He'd always believed that his father should have taken the throne for himself when he had had the chance. He also had no love for Tostig, whom he had considered a rival since they were boys.

Harold frowned.

"Surely he will. Already his indecision has attracted the attentions of William of Normandy, not to mention others." Harold replied.

A Norman ambassador had arrived in the city only days before to express Williams claim to the crown. Mercifully the nobles who met with the man had scorned the idea that William had any right to take the throne of England. In Saxon law what the king said on his deathbed took precedence over any oath that had been made several years previously. The Norman had left in a rage and had promised that the matter was not over.

Harold winced at the memory of his capture in Normandy several years previously. The humiliation he had felt as he knelt to William and lied through his teeth to be his man and to ensure the Duke was made King. To Harold what he had said was not an oath but a necessary speech to leave Normandy alive. It was obvious to him now though that William had taken it all very seriously.

Gyrth nudged Harold out of his thoughts. Across the room one of the monks was waving at him to approach the Kings bed. Harold's heart rate quickened in anticipation, this was it surely?

Gyrth winked at his brother as Harold walked over to the bed. The smell of death was almost overwhelming. He pushed his way through the group of clergymen and knelt at the Kings side. On the other side of the bed stood Queen Edith her face a mask of distress and utter misery. She dabbed a damp silken cloth onto her husband's forehead and whispered soothing words into his ear.

"My king, I am here." Harold said.

For a long time the King remained silent, his eyes closed. All of a sudden he let out a cry and his eyes snapped open startling Harold and the other people standing around the bed.

"Sire?" Harold asked cautiously.

Edward's head turned to face him, his eyes large and filled with fear. A fear that now wormed its way into Harold's guts.

"God has shown me our end!" the king suddenly yelled out. "The Devil will consume this land with sword and flame!"

The people around the bed stepped back, all except Harold who leaned in closer to the king. The queen cried out and wept as her dying husband ranted on.

"God is angry with my people; o' lord protect them all, they must repent for their wickedness! Forgive them!"

The king raved on in delirium for several minutes before he finally fell quiet. Edith wept and lamented in the corner of the room and was comforted by the priests and bishops.

"He is a prophet from God!" she cried as she was led out of the chamber.

Harold simply stayed kneeling and stared at the man who was his king.

"The ravings of a scared dying man brother, nothing more." Gyrth whispered as he stood next to his brother. Harold nodded in silent agreement. He didn't doubt his brother's words but the sense of dread twisted tighter.

Edward opened his eyes once more, the madness that had been in them now gone and replaced by clarity. The ailing man looked at Harold and smiled faintly.

"We have been through much together, you and I Lord Harold. Please bring my wife and the clergymen back into my chamber I must speak."

Harold gestured to Gyrth who with a bow left the chamber to retrieve the Kings distressed wife. Harold and Edward were left alone, an awkward silence lingering between them.

"He hates you." Edward said weakly, referring to Tostig.

"I know." Harold replied sadly.

"Your own brother will be your undoing."

Harold nodded in agreement. He regretted all that had transpired between himself and Tostig and knew that one day soon there would be a reckoning. Harold was about to speak when the others returned to the room, he held his tongue.

Edith took her husband's hand and knelt at his side. She still wept but Edward persevered.

"Almighty God, please repay my wife for her love and dutiful service to me, this will be my last will and testament." he croaked.

The king took hold of Harold's hand. "I commend this woman and the entire kingdom to your protection. Remember that she is your lady and sister and serve faithfully and honour her as such for the all the days of her life. I proclaim you as protector of all Huscarl's and foreign servants."

The king spoke on but Harold heard none of the rest. Finally the throne was his. He was the named heir and under Saxon law the last words of the king superseded any previous oaths.

William the bastard had no legitimate claim to the kingdom; surely the man would not follow up with his threats?

***

15.

April 1066

Driffield

Osfrid gazed out to sea from his vantage point on the palisades watchtower. The weather was finally turning. The sky was still a menacing grey, and the sea rolled and tumbled in violent spasms, but at last the wind had turned. Winter was receding and the hope of spring was in the air.

He wore a long leather jerkin over his woollen leggings and deer hide boots. His hair was longer than it had ever been, now resting past his shoulders; he refused to cut it until he held his wife and daughter in his arms once more.

Since the death of Edward he had spent the past three months assembling a crew for the ship he had moored just off the coast. Only the thought of finally setting sail had kept him going throughout those long dark days.

Acca and the others had busied themselves by training with Hunweld and his small contingent of Varangian's, the sound of clashing metal and the sharpening of blades had rang out through the winter.

"Osfrid?" the voice of his father stirred him from his thoughts. The big man climbed the rickety ladder and stood next to his son.

"Very soon we will set sail. It should be another week, by our good captains reckoning."

Osfrid nodded pleased at the news.

"Good. How are the men coming along?" he asked as he waved to his son who was helping Ceadda carry a basket of food up the hill.

"They are all capable, but I doubt many will last long against a Viking Berserker. Except of course my Varangian's and there are few enough of them." Hunweld paused for a moment causing Osfrid to look at his father questioningly.

" Acca, now he has potential to become a great warrior. You were very lucky to meet him. A few more years and he might even be able to give you a run for his money." He chuckled.

"He has proven himself to be loyal beyond measure." Agreed Osfrid; 'I made him a part of my household garrison, he deserves better than being a simple spearman."

*

April

North Sea

The merciless rocking of the grey and pitiless sea made the hardened warriors of Byzantium sick to their stomachs. The Varangian's were all capable sailors but they were used to the calmer seas of the Mediterranean or Baltic.

Osfrid and the other Saxons too were constantly running to the small ships rail and emptying the contents of their stomachs over the side. Only the old sea captain who Acca had met the week before was enjoying the ride. He chuckled as he watched men far younger than himself show their true sea legs.

The ship, which was a similar design to the fearsome Nordic Longboats, was called the *Kelsi* which was the Saxon word for ship victory. It had cost Osfrid a large sum of coin to loan the ship from the Kings navy but after all that he had done to get the northern earls to support Harold as King he'd expected the price not to have been quite so high.

Osfrid gripped the rail and wretched as once more the sea rocked the boat wildly. Acca staggered to his side and he too emptied his stomach.

"Bloody old fool." He moaned, speaking of the old captain who was cackling at the sight of two of the Varangian's collapsing to the deck in misery. "He told me that the sea would be calm!" Acca raised a fist in the air and shook it in mock anger at the captain.

Osfrid chuckled.

"This is the earliest we could set sail Acca, I expected the journey would be a little rough.' He paused as he almost lost his footing. 'But I didn't expect it to be as rough as this."

Sea water had drenched them all as towering waves threatened to engulf them. Osfrid now had a deep respect for the Viking raiders of old. Whoever could endure such journeys immediately rose in his expectations.

He wiped his hand through his beard; he straightened up again and frowned as he looked to the distant horizon. Somewhere over there, was his wife and daughter. He would hold them in his arms again, of that he was certain. If not, then Gods have mercy on any who stood in his way.

He looked around at the men who were willing to follow him into peril. Sailing to a hostile kingdom on pirate infested waters was not his idea of a good time, and yet they had come. A feeling of pride and love for his comrades filled him.

Standing next to him and in the middle of a mock argument was Acca, the young man who he had liberated from Morcar several months before. In that time the man had proven himself to be loyal beyond measure; he had been willing to risk his life to save the family of a man he had hardly known, even coming close to death at the hand of Tostig's henchmen. Osfrid smiled as his young friend threatened to throw the cackling captain overboard. In the days to come he knew that he would be able to rely on him.

Ceadda, his most trustful servant was at one of the oars. His massive arms betraying not a sign of weakness as he and the Varangian's propelled the ship along its journey. Osfrid had known him since he himself was a young lad. It had been Ceadda that had taught him how to fight with an axe and to ride a horse. Osfrid had wanted his steward to stay in Driffield to protect his son but the older man had insisted. He blamed himself for losing Aerlene and Esma.

He took some comfort that Cearl was watching over Wulf whilst they were away. Since York he had become good friends with the Thegn and since the murder of Cearl's family at Tostig's hands the sad and lonely man had spent more and more time at Driffield.

At the ships oars were his father's men the Varangian's. Over the few days since they had arrived at Driffield he had grown to like these foreigners. Standing over them like a protective parent was his father.

He had led them for over a decade against the distant Empires enemies.

He wore his full battle armour, at a distance he would look like a war god shining in his armoured glory. He wore a coat of mail that had polished to a dazzlingly shine over which he wore his red cloak emblazoned with the two headed eagle of Byzantium. His helmet was iron plated with gold cheek pieces and a plume of large eagle feathers.

It was a good plan, for any pirates seeking an easy catch would be put off from attacking a vessel bearing such a fearsome looking warrior.

Osfrid gingerly made his way over to his father and sat down on a small wooden bench. Behind him lay their equipment, swords, axes and armour were neatly stowed away and covered in cloth to protect them from the corrosive effects of sea water.

"Our captain reckons we should make landfall in another three days."Hunweld said as he drank a swig from a water cask. He offered the cask to Osfrid who greedily gulped the sweet water, washing away the taste of bile from the back of his throat.

"Good, I don't know how much more of this sea the men can take." Osfrid muttered. Hunweld laughed. "These Varangian can handle the sea lad. They've fought battles in rougher seas than this."

Osfrid was curious about his father's exploits in the East and since his return to England they hadn't had much time to talk.

"Tell me about it." Osfrid asked.

Hunweld drank another gulp before tossing the cask to one of his men on the oars.

"I know that I have been gone a long time son. As you know I didn't handle your mother's death well." Hunweld replied sadly his eyes taking on a distant look. 'I couldn't stay in England. Edward and his bastard Norman kin made me sick to my stomach. It was Earl Godwin that suggested I leave you know." He raised an eyebrow as he told Osfrid. 'The wretch believed I'd cause too much trouble for the little wimp. And he would have been proven right if I had stayed." he chuckled.

This revelation was a surprise to Osfrid. He had just believed that his father had left to escape the memories of his beloved wife. He nodded as Hunweld continued.

"I arrived in Constantinople just as news of the Emperor Michael's death was announced. The place was in an uproar and only by bribing my way through the gate did I meet my contact.

'The following months were strange as civil war erupted throughout the empire. Several nobles were after the throne you see, and chaos was breaking out.'

"Sounds familiar." Osfrid muttered.

'Luckily for me, at that time I had been stationed to Anatolia with the Varangian's. We were under the command of a man named Isaac Comenus. He was the man who recognised my leadership and who made me a captain.

'I and my men captured a small Arab patrol that was carrying important orders to their commander. Using what we had captured Isaac led his army to victory in battle several days later.

'Funnily enough two years later that man Isaac took the throne for himself and was made *Basileus,* Emperor in our tongue. Sadly though that great man died not long after and was replaced by a fool called Constantine Ducas."

Hunweld shrugged his shoulders in regret.

"When I left he was still in charge. God knows what state the Empire is in under his care."

Osfrid was about to ask more questions about the Empire that sounded so strange to him when the old sea captain caught his attention.

"Sails sighted." The captain cried, pointing frantically to the horizon. Osfrid bounded over to the ships side and squinted against the sunlight, sure enough two sails were there. His stomach sank as he saw the two ships change course.

"They're heading our way." Acca called out nervously.

"Viking pirates" the old captain snarled.

With every passing second the ships were getting closer, now they could be clearly seen, a sight that had brought nightmares to Saxons for generations, Longboats.

Their prows each bore the fearsome figure of a snarling beast and their decks were filled with men hastily equipping themselves with armour and weaponry.

***

16.

The old captain hurried down the ship yelling at the oarsmen to pick up the pace.

"Row you buggers row!" he yelled.

The Varangian's threw all of their muscle power into moving the heavy wooden oars through the water. The little ship lurched slightly as it picked up speed. Osfrid quickly strapped on his armour and fastened his sword belt. He hefted his Dragon hilted sword and did three quick swipes. It was good to hold it, reassuring. Acca had joined the Varangian's at the oars whilst Hunweld barked shouts of encouragement to his men.

As every minute passed the two longboats got closer. The rhythmic chanting of their crews was carried on the wind unnerving the Saxons. An hour passed and Osfrid could see that the crew was growing tired, they were men meant for battle not to row.

Dark ominous clouds were gathering in the distance and land was too far away for them to reach before their pursuers caught them. He tightened his grip on his sword and picked up his large round shield. He caught his father's eye and nodded. Hunweld smiled back glad to have the decision made. He stood and yelled to the men.

"We cannot outrun these pirate dogs. Take up your weapons and armour. Let's give them a welcome they will never forget."

The Varangian's roared as one and quickly got their weapons. The odds were definitely not on their side. The smaller Saxon ship was carrying only sixteen warriors. A few scared oarsmen and the old sea captain. The two longboats were carrying forty warriors apiece, their cheers and abuse carried clearly across the rough sea.

Osfrid could see the longboats drawing ever closer, he could now make out the men on their decks.

Fearsome blonde haired Vikings adorned in battle dress filled the decks. He made a prayer to the Gods for their deliverance. His wife may believe in the Christ god but he had always preferred the old ways of his ancestors.

Grapple lines soared through the air and with a sickening crunch the Saxon ship was caught by the nearer Longboat. Slowly, the little ship was hauled closer and closer to the pirates.

"Face the first ship. Deal with these wretches then we shall worry about the other." Hunweld roared.

The ships smashed together sending splinters flying and causing waves of water to surge between the two ships, soaking the Saxons.

Several pirates launched themselves into the attack, jumping from their ship to the other, axes and swords swinging. Osfrid saw one of the Saxon oarsmen cut down but with devastating speed a Varangian swung his axe decapitating the raider with one fell blow.

The battle had begun.

More and more of the pirates attempted to board the little ship but the Varangian's locked shields and batted them backwards. Osfrid plunged into the fray thrusting and stabbing as he went. His shield rocked from an axe blow sending pain shooting up his arm. To his left he could see Acca wrestling one of the pirates and using his strength to throw his foe into the dark churning water. The Varangian's held fast as they defended the ships side.

Blood covered the decks and ran in a river down the row of oars. Finally the weight of sheer numbers forced them to step backwards. Now the fight became a pushing match, one side desperate to prevent the other from boarding their vessel.

The violent rocking motion threatened to capsize both vessels and would have if not for Ceadda cutting the longboats grapple line with his axe.

"Look out!" shouted the old captain who was brandishing a blood soaked axe in his wrinkly hands. Osfrid spun and saw a second grapple line attach itself to the boat. The other Longboat had arrived.

"Fight back to back." He yelled and the Varangian's expertly folded their makeshift shield wall so that they divided into two. Now they faced outwards on both sides of the ship. Acca and Hunweld fought desperately as Osfrid turned to face the new threat. Ceadda ducked as a hurled axe narrowly missed his head and embedded itself into the deck beneath him. He swore violently cursing his enemies.

"Don't know how we're going to get out of this one milord." He snarled savagely.

Osfrid tensed himself as the second Longboat smashed into his own ship. The motion rocked the smaller ship sending the Varangian's sprawling and sending their attackers flailing into the sea, some were crushed between their own ship and their prey. Screams reverberated through the air and the sickening crunch of men being turned to pulp almost made Osfrid wretch.

Two more grapples latched themselves onto the Saxon ship which Ceadda set about hacking away.

It was too late.

A dozen armoured Vikings leapt aboard shoving the Varangian's back and clearing a space for their comrades. Osfrid and his men reacted immediately his sword slashing left and right, his shield battering his attackers back over the railing.

An axe blade smashed into the side of his helmet sending him staggering onto his knees, he shut his eyes awaiting the blow that would surely finish him. Acca stepped in front of his lord, taking the killer blow onto his heavy shield and stabbed back with his own blade piercing the Vikings armour and sending the man screaming into the sea. He offered Osfrid his hand which was gratefully taken, and hauled his master back onto his feet.

"We're holding the bastards." Hunweld yelled from the opposite side of the deck. The first Longboat was now drifting away from the Saxons, its grapple lines all cut and its decks filled with wounded angry Vikings. The sea surrounding the battle was crimson with the bodies of Vikings drifting in the rough currents.

Osfrid was filled with relief that one of their foes was out of the way licking its wounds but now he and his men had to repeat the feat of driving off a ship of angry warriors. Hunweld and Ceadda now joined Acca and Osfrid in defending against the fresh longboat.

Axes swung, Swords sliced and shields splintered as the skirmish raged on. Hours passed before the two sides disengaged. Both forces were exhausted.

The Vikings glared at the Saxons, who in turn stared straight back tensed and ready to fight until the very end.

Osfrid gasped for breath, his arms ached and he was bleeding from numerous small wounds. During the furious fighting he hadn't been able to see what casualties had been taken but now he did. All of the Saxon sailors were strewn on the deck dead. The old sea captain was too, a sword had buried itself deep into the man's chest.

Acca handed his lord a flask of water and sat heavily onto the deck. He reeked of sweat and blood.

"The captain's dead milord." Acca said sadly.

Osfrid gulped the water greedily before handing the flask back to his young servant.

"Without him we won't be able to reach the Norwegian coast. None of us still standing know these waters." He replied frustrated.

Osfrid walked over to his father who was still in the shield wall with his men.

"Father, we only have two choices left to us." He explained as he glared at the Vikings. The first longboat had drifted far away during the hours of battle and was now just a speck on the horizon.

"We either storm their ship and hope to capture it with some of its crew alive or we surrender and risk being slaughtered."

Hunweld looked around at the bodies of the captain, and the other sailors and, swore. His Varangian's were close to exhaustion despite the steel in their eyes. What he decided to do next could kill them all, but what choice did they have?

"We're not surrendering." He answered his son flatly.

"Then a charge it is." Osfrid replied. He stretched his aching limbs and joined the Varangian's.

*

Acca and Ceadda looked at each in disbelief.

"Were going to attack?" Acca whispered to his friend.

"Aye lad looks like it. Fight likes the devil and the lord above shall see us through." Ceadda whispered back.

Acca gulped loudly.

*

The grim faced Saxons bellowed a challenge catching the Vikings by surprise. They stood there disbelievingly hoping that their foe would surely surrender. The Vikings had watched as the small band of Saxons had mauled their sister ships crew and had tasted the metal of their swords themselves. Out of forty warriors only thirty remained, whereas the Varangian's had not lost a single warrior.

All of a sudden the band of Saxons exploded over the bow of their ship and launched themselves into the Viking lines.

The Varangian's moved forward methodically swinging their axes and swords cutting down scores of the pirates.

Osfrid's heart raced with excitement. The savagery of their assault had had its desired effect. The Vikings panicked as their shield wall buckled sending many of them jumping overboard to escape the deadly sting of their enemy's weapons. Those that jumped instantly sank under the waves as their heavy chainmail armour dragged them down into the icy depths.

"Disengage." Hunweld commanded. At once the Varangian's halted their attack.

To Osfrid's surprise only a dozen Vikings remained standing, their weapons thrown to the deck or overboard. Acca and Ceadda rushed forward and pushed their captives onto their knees where they found some rope and tied the prisoner's hands.

A loud crashing caused Osfrid to turn. The smaller Saxon ship had been flooded with sea water during the attack and now finally the weight of the water had caused it to flounder.

With a snap the mast buckled, the bottom split and the little boat sank beneath the waves.

He put his hand on Acca's chest preventing the young man from trying to save the stricken vessel.

"No lad. She served her purpose and lived up to her name." They had achieved *Kelsi* the sea victory.

***

17.

Three weeks passed before the Saxons arrived on the shores of Norway. Their captives proved to be impressive seamen, bringing their longboat through a terrible storm that lasted a whole four days and nights. Supplies hadn't been an issue as the longboat had been fully stocked to provide for forty men instead of twenty.

The Varangian's and the surviving Vikings rowed the ship into the mouth of a narrow river where they beached the vessel.

Osfrid jumped over the low riding side into waist deep and freezing water. Acca followed, doing his best to keep the bundles of weapons out of the corrosive sea. As his feet reached dry land Osfrid fell to his knees and kissed the sand. He threw his head back and laughed.

"We live!" he shouted towards the heavens. The rest of his men followed suite, relief evident on their faces.

"Acca, go inshore and take some of the Varangian's with you, find us a place to make camp, be quick now lad, night is falling." Hunweld barked, his experience of surviving in hostile territory overwhelming his sense of relief.

Acca waved at some of the men to follow and they ran up the sloping shingle beach disappearing into the tree line.

Osfrid turned to see Ceadda and the remaining Varangian's start unloading the ship.

"It cost us dearly." He said bitterly.

Hunweld slapped his son on the back before standing next to him.

"Aye, it was. But those Saxon boys knew what was at stake. They died for you, Osfrid, their lord." He replied soothingly. "Now we have to decide what to do with our Norse friends over there." He added, gesturing to the captive pirates who were now once more bound at their hands and kneeling in the sand, watched by a steely eyed Varangian, his axe held at the ready in case they caused any mischief.

Osfrid frowned in thought stroking his long blonde beard in concentration. His mind made up, he walked purposefully over to the trembling and terrified captives. He raised his voice and spoke harshly so that the Norwegians could not mistake what he was about to say.

"We cannot take them with us. Men such as those are not to be trusted, kill them." Osfrid nodded to the Varangian who stepped up behind the first prisoner, he raised his axe high and brought it down onto the screaming man's neck. The pitiful cry was cut short as the heavy axe blade struck severing muscle and bone causing the pirate to crumple into the sand. A pool of blood seeped out from the corpse.

The Varangian moved onto the next captive and the next, dispatching each with the same remorseless poise. He stepped up behind the last pirate who unlike the others was not screaming out in fear. The Viking had his head held high staring defiantly at Osfrid. Then to Osfrid's surprise the man spoke in Anglisc.

"I do not fear death Saxon. I have faced it many times."

The Varangian hesitated as the man spoke giving his intended victim the time he needed to swiftly rise to his feet. The Viking swung his tied fists smashing them into the Varangian's nose like a club, breaking it with a sickening crunch. He cut his bonds on his would be executioners axe which he then ripped out of the wounded man's hands. He raised it high, about to bring the blade down in a killing strike; the Varangian had collapsed onto the shingle grasping his bleeding nose, powerless against the crazed Viking. The axe fell.

With a clang of metal Hunweld took the deadly blow on the tip of his sword causing the axe head to narrowly miss its intended target. Seeing his chance the wounded Varangian scrambled away from his attacker before being helped by his comrades.

Now Hunweld and the Viking stood facing one another. The Saxon adorned in his armoured magnificence, the Viking in nothing but a torn tunic and breaches.

"Very Impressive, for a Viking turd." Hunweld joked looking at the younger man with a sense of admiration. He waved at his men to stand down.

The one thing that Hunweld admired above all things was a man's bravery and skill in battle. It had taken Osfrid years to earn that respect. At fifteen he had slain his first enemy soldier, a raider from the North who had been terrorising the local populace. It had been a good fight, the fight that had resulted in his broken nose and a deep scar on his chest. Both could be seen today albeit, the nose had healed over time, and the scar was now just one of many.

The Viking yelled as he charged bringing the axe down at Hunweld's feet. The older warrior easily parried before launching a series of quick stabs forcing the Viking to dance backwards up the beach. Osfrid kept pace with the fighters as they moved. Minutes passed as neither combatant could find a way through the others guard.

Hunweld swung his sword in a mighty arc but the Viking nimbly danced out of its reach causing the older man to laugh.

"It's been many a year since a man has proven to be such a challenge." He said in genuine admiration. "Who taught you to fight lad?"

The Viking had his hands on his knees gasping for air; the fight had been fast and tiring.

"My father taught me. He was a great warrior. He was a Varangian." The younger man said with pride.

Hunweld lowered his sword but remained tensed and ready to defend himself.

"Your father was a Varangian? Lad, I and my men are Varangian's. You, 'he said pointing his sword, 'are nothing but a bastard pirate." The Viking likewise lowered his weapon at Hunweld's revelation.

"My father fought at the side of King Harald Hardrada when he served the Empire against the Infidels. He brought much honour to my family.' He paused and a look of anger creased his features. 'He was betrayed by the king and we were forced into banditry to survive."

"How come you speak Anglisc?" asked Osfrid who had been watching the exchange with interest. He knew that his small band of men could use a native Norwegian to help them find his family, this young Viking looked promising.

The Viking turned to face him "My mother was Saxon. A slave captured during a raid years and years ago."

"So you are part Saxon. What is your name?" Osfrid asked.

"Ragner Oakenson." The Viking replied.

Hunweld sheathed his sword and encouraged Ragner to drop the axe he still held firmly in his grasp.

After a few moments hesitation Ragner relented and threw his weapon to the ground. Osfrid walked forward and picked up the weapon, he threw the axe to a Varangian.

"Well Ragner Oakenson, do you know the way to Oslo from here?" He asked.

Ragner looked around at the landscape. To the north were foothills surrounded by a mist, to the East lay the river that the longboat had entered. After a few minutes deep in thought the Viking smiled.

"Aye I know the way from here. It should be a six day walk to the North East.' He hesitated before continuing;' If I lead you there, will you promise to let me live?"

Hunweld spoke with his son.

"I think we have no choice but to trust him, none of us buggers knows the way, and it wouldn't hurt to have another dangerous bastard in our little group."

Osfrid nodded in agreement.

"Aye, that is true father. Just promise me you won't be filling his head with tales of your deeds and the glory of the Varangian's all the way there." He replied cautiously.

With it agreed the two men turned and faced Ragner.

"Agreed Ragner Oakenson, you guide us to Oslo and to my family and I promise to let you live", Osfrid said seriously.

*

The band of warriors spoke in hushed tones around the fire that Acca had made. They had walked deeper into the woods after they had secured the longboat in the beaches tree line.

Ceadda had prepared a meal of venison and dried bread. The deer he had killed earlier that evening as the band traipsed through the foliage. Acca munched greedily into the tasty meat, hard labour always made him ravenous. He frowned as his gaze fell on the Viking that Osfrid had spared. The man was probably the same age as himself but the blue eyes told a different story. It told of a life of hardship, of one filled with nefarious and dishonest deeds.

To Acca the Viking felt like some sort of evil twin of himself. He noticed that Hunweld was deep in conversation with the man, the quiet chatter sometimes broken by a laugh from the old man. Inside, he felt a pang of jealousy; Acca had hoped that the fearsome old warrior would teach him more of the ways of combat and of the Eastern Empire. Now it seemed he'd found a new favourite.

Osfrid came out of the shadows and crouched down next to him.

"Acca, I have a task for you." He whispered.

Acca looked at his master.

"Of course lord, anything." Acca replied through another mouthful of venison.

Osfrid took a bite out of the piece of bread he was holding. He chewed for a moment, all the while looking at the young man chatting with his father.

"I want you to keep an eye on our guide there. I don't trust him."

Acca nodded in understanding, he was glad his master saw the possible dangers of having a man who could betray them in their midst.

*

18.

April 1066

Norway

The band of warriors slowly wound their way through the spectacular scenery of the Norwegian fjords, and massive forests. Trees higher than many of them had ever seen before, and in such numbers that it boggled the mind. For three days they had walked without pause, save for a few hours each night, when the lack of light made the narrow paths treacherous.

Ragner seemed to know the country like the back of his hands, only once had they had gotten lost. They hugged close to the well-worn dirt roads that lead to the port of Oslo. They had daren't not use them directly in case they should stumble onto a Norse patrol, or run into bandits that frequented the isolated trails. Every man was footsore and hungry, and out of the number that had started two had had to drop out and return to the ship. One had been the Varangian whose nose had been badly broken by Ragner in his attempted escape. The big Rus couldn't carry on due to being unable to breathe properly. Blood continually clogged up his nose making it impossible for him to keep up.

In some ways Osfrid was glad that they now had someone guarding the ship, he figured that if it came to a confrontation his men would be outnumbered anyway regardless of how many troops he had. Osfrid had ordered one of the other Varangian's to go with the wounded man. Nothing was worse than being left behind alone.

His memory recalled an incident from his youth, when he had been new to the ways of battle. He had been sixteen when he and a small war band had been sent to the Scottish border; there they had been harassed by the painted warriors all through their campaign. He had been injured on a march and had been told to wait for the others in a small valley and to keep hidden. He'd done his best but somehow the savages had found him. For three days and nights he had ran in fear from the savage chants of the Scots tribesmen.

On a quiet night he could still hear that terrible chant in his mind.

Despite the coming of the spring a chill hung in the air. Each of the men was wearing heavy animal hide cloaks and gloves. Night was falling once again and within the hour Hunweld called a halt for the night. Acca and the others immediately set about making a fire whilst Ceadda began handing out supplies of dried mutton and stale bread. Osfrid thanked the older man, biting eagerly into the food. Hunweld waved him over to where he, Ragner and three of the Varangian's were huddled together.

"Ragner has a plan for us to get inside the town." Hunweld explained. Who was crouching over a pile of sticks, trying unsuccessfully to start a fire. 'These are my best men that speak Nordic" he added pointing to the Varangian's present.

Osfrid took out a piece of flint from his pocket and started the fire with one strike from his dagger. Sparks erupted immediately setting the pile ablaze.

"Move over old man." Chuckled Osfrid as he nudged his father out of the way, he blew onto the flame feeding it with his breath.

Once the fire was suitably ablaze he stood up and chucked a few more twigs and leaves onto the flame. He faced Ragner. "So what is this plan?"

Ragner didn't flinch under Osfrid's stern gaze, most men did. For that he had earned a little bit of respect in Osfrid's eyes.

Ragner rubbed his jaw in thought.

"The town is protected by a wall and palisades, with the harbour being guarded by a wall and tower. Archers and spearmen are ever vigilant. After Hardrada's war with Denmark the ports are vulnerable to attack."

Hunweld laughed.

"Vikings being raped and pillaged by Vikings, oh the irony." The men chuckled.

Ragner frowned in annoyance, remaining silent until Hunweld urged him to continue.

The young Viking cleared his throat.

"Your men will stand out like a priest in a brothel. If you cannot speak Norse then you will be caught. I and these men can get inside the town and get you lot in."

Osfrid nodded in agreement, so far the plan sounded obviously simple.

"Our main task is to locate the slave master Olaf Fork-beard. Then we can find my wife and daughter." Osfrid explained. He waved Ceadda over. The big man had finished his task and was practicing with his axe. The mighty axe swung through the air in ever tightening circles, it was dazzling to behold. The big man finished his swings and delicately placed the weapon against the trunk of a pine.

"How can I be of service lords?"

Hunweld raised an eyebrow and told his old friend to stop being so bloody polite.
Osfrid smiled with the others.

"You saw the men who took my family. How many were there? He asked.

Ceadda crouched down next to the fire and warmed his hands in the flames heat. He thought for a few moments, the brief fight on the Northumbrian beach flashed back into his mind.

"There were two men waiting on the beach, a massive man and some spindly little weasel of a man. A boat full of Viking berserkers arrived to pick them up. I killed the big man, but it was the other that took Lady Aerlene and Ms Esma."

Handel. That was the man Ceadda was describing.

Osfrid's thoughts went to a dark place thinking about what he would do to the fetcher when he caught up to him.

It wasn't until midnight that the men had agreed on their course of action. It had been decided that Ragner and three of the Varangian's would go on ahead into Oslo and locate the slave master Olav. Osfrid and the other Saxons would then sneak into the town thanks to Ragner and liberate the slaves.

The remaining eight Varangian's would be sent back to the ship and get it ready to sail in a weeks' time. If all went to plan then they would be able to rescue the family and escape by sea.

After the meeting Osfrid found a spot under a tree and looked at the night's sky. He frowned as he saw a bright object moving slowly overhead. A long tail trailed white across the sky, He crossed himself in fear. A bad omen if ever there was one.

***

19.

May 1066

Palace of Westminster

Harold stared at the young messenger standing nervously before him. He could barely contain his anger at the news. It was bad enough that his treacherous brother had sacked and raided the south coast, raised an army of Flemish mercenaries and occupied the Isle of Wight. Now the pox faced man before him had delivered even graver news.

William of Normandy was preparing for war. Even worse, the wretch had persuaded his holiness the pope to back his campaign. England was now the target of a religious Crusade and now his priests had warned him of Gods displeasure, the comet trailing through the sky had spread terror throughout his superstitious people.

The throne on which he sat was made of the finest wood covered in a purple velvet cloth and cushion. It wasn't very comfortable. He stood and stretched his legs, the morning's meetings had dragged on for hours, he yearned to escape, to go hunting, and to try to forget the troubles that were plaguing his short reign. He had yearned to be king for many years, not knowing the burdens it involved. The news from Europe was troubling. Knights and warriors from across the continent would flock to William's banner. A small consolation was that it was apparent that William believed he could not invade on his own.

Harold took off his crown and twirled it around on his finger. He was deep in thought.

"The pope has sanctioned his actions?" he asked again.

The nervous messenger nodded vigorously.

"Y-yes my lord. The duke has already welcomed mercenaries from Italia and Germany. It is said that he has ordered the construction of a massive fleet to bring them across the channel."

Harold smiled slightly. 'It will take him months to be fully prepared. I have time.' He thought. Anger seethed inside him, the pope had ignored his own messenger who had been sent to persuade the pontiff that the troubles of England were not Rome's concern. Obviously the voice of God had been bribed by Normandy.

He waved the messenger away and handed the crown to a servant who had been waiting patiently beside the throne.

He waved Gyrth over to him. His brother had been a stalwart ally in the troubled early days of his reign.

Already he had heard whispers of discontent from the Northern nobles. Morcar and his brother were stirring up dissent in Northumbria; he would have to put them back into their places very soon.

"Brother." Gyrth said bowing to his king. Harold put his hands on his brother's shoulders.

"Take a ship and drive Tostig away. For too long I've let him roam unchecked."

Gyrth nodded. If he had it his way he would have locked their traitorous brother away for life.

"What should I do if I catch him?"

Harold thought for a moment.

"Kill him." He replied simply; his voice full of sadness.

Gyrth nodded in understanding before bowing and leaving the hall. Harold sighed, and waved the other gathered courtiers out of the chamber before he himself walked out; two of his Huscarl's fell into step on either side of him. Each wore full mail and was armed with the Saxon sword known as equalisers. The long swords were lethal, allowing extra reach and capable of delivering powerful cuts.

After walking through the palace Harold reached his chambers leaving his bodyguards to stand guard outside.

He closed the oak door and sighed heavily. His mistress Edith rushed to him embracing him tightly.

"My love what troubles thee?" She asked softly. Harold nuzzled her neck, kissing his way down it. It wasn't for nothing that the courtiers nicknamed her the '*swan neck*'.

"I have many enemies and few friends." He whispered into her ear brushing her long golden hair.

Edith took his hand and led him to the bed pushing him softly down onto the soft mattress.

"You are king; to be king is to have no friends. You can trust in men but you alone can rule supreme." She replied seductively. She hitched her dress and straddled her king untying his breeches as she did so. She slid down his torso causing him to moan with pleasure.

"The kingdoms troubles can wait, at least for an afternoon." Harold said breathlessly as she pleasured him.

*

20.

Isle of Wight

Tostig watched as the fires raged and the women screamed. Since his exile he had done whatever he could to get vengeance on his brother. His first port of call had been Scotland where he had taken refuge with his friend King Malcolm.

After that he had set sail for Flanders, and using the gold he had been given had hired several hundred Flemish mercenaries. With them, he had ravaged the coast of England, burning and pillaging as they went. Frustratingly however, he hadn't drawn his brother out to face him. Now he stood on the Isle of Wight. Its settlements were put to the torch and its inhabitants slaughtered or enslaved. His men eagerly took anything of value. Since joining with him those men had gotten rich from raiding.

He turned and stood unmoving as a young woman was dragged out of her home and raped before him. Her pitiful cries only fed his anger and lust for vengeance. Frustration was threatening to overwhelm him. He had travelled to Normandy to convince William to launch an invasion immediately. The duke had dismissed the notion, that he would take his time and prepare, he had urged Tostig to patience. But patient was one thing Tostig wasn't.

The woman was writhing against her attacker, clawing at the burly man's face. The soldier laughed in her face, his mates egging him on.

A shout of warning came from one of the lookouts. Tostig faced the sea and saw some of his ships take to sea in a panic. He scowled against the sunlight; there on the misty horizon were sails. Five of them were flying the flag of the Kings navy.

He cupped his mouth and bellowed at his men to return to the ships. Raping and pillaging was one thing, battling an army was another. The Flemish mercenaries raping the girl stopped, the man on the girl drew his dagger and cut her throat remorselessly before wiping it clean on his coat. The men laughed as they jogged towards the boats. Tostig smiled as he gazed at the carnage he had inflicted onto Harold's subjects. He was capable of so much more, if only he could find another man to match his ambition for quick justice.

***

21.

Oslo

The ravenous squawking of seagulls and the stench of fresh fish gave away that they were close to the bustling port of Oslo. The small band had walked for a further four days since the plan was decided upon. The eight Varangian's had departed that night back towards the ship. In another few days they should have sailed the ship closer to the port. Osfrid had given them some gold to be used to bribe any local they came across to aid them in navigating the route.

Now there was just himself, his father, Acca, Ceadda, Ragner and the three remaining Varangian's. They had crept closer to the port during the night and had set up camp on a hill overlooking the harbour. The sails of dozens of fishing and trading vessels could be seen travelling to and from the place.

Docked in the harbour itself were dozens of other ships of varying sizes. Longboats were beached on the shoreline waiting to be repaired or painted and the hammering of carpenters could clearly be heard.

Dawn had arrived an hour previously and Acca who had been watching the town gate trotted into the camp.

"The guards have opened the gates; they're letting in merchants and traveller's now." He reported breathlessly.

Hunweld told his men to prepare. Each of the Varangian's stripped out of their armour and donned travellers cloaks and tunics. They gave their axes to Ceadda who placed them into a sack which he then buried under a tree. The only weapons they had on them were daggers and swords.

"All is ready?" asked Ragner. He too wore a cloak and was armed with a dagger tucked into his boot. The Varangian's replied in the affirmative.

"Once we've located Olaf we will light a fire there." Ragner pointed to a disused stone structure at the edge of town.

"Once the fire is lit make your way to the East gate, we will wait for you there."

Osfrid shook the young Vikings hand.

"Thank you. I will owe you much when this is over."

Ragner smiled.

"Why else do you think I'm doing this?" he joked. He turned pulling up the hood on his cloak before walking off down the hill. The Varangian's followed chatting amongst themselves.
Acca scowled at Ragner as he walked passed. He stopped the Viking, gripping his arm.

"You'd best not betray us." Acca warned quietly. Ragner laughed mockingly and shook himself free before carrying on his way.

*

It was another two days before the fire was lit. Ceadda had been on the second night watch and woke the others. Those two days had been nerve wracking; questions kept floating into Osfrid's mind. Had they been caught? Betrayed?

Each of them quickly got dressed and armed before hurriedly making their way down the treacherous slope towards the town. The moon was high and bright in the sky lighting their way.

Stealthily they made towards the Eastern gate, careful not to make too much noise and to avoid any patrolling guards.

They reached the gate with no fuss except for Acca falling over in the darkness. Now they crouched in the tree line watching the gate. Two Norse guards stood at either side of it. Behind them, silently climbing over the wall was two of the Varangian's. With amazing skill they silently dropped down and dispatched the guards, dragging them rapidly into the undergrowth. A few moments later they reappeared now wearing the guards armour. To an untrained eye the two men taking up position were the genuine sentries. With a creek, the gate swung open. The third Varangian stood in the opening holding a flaming torch, he whistled the all clear. Osfrid and the others stood and ran quickly toward the gate. Once they were all inside the two 'guardsmen' closed the gate behind them.

"Where's Ragner?" Hunweld asked the Varangian who'd open the gate.

The warrior looked nervous.

"I don't know lord. He disappeared into the town once we got inside."

Acca swore under his breath. "I knew he wasn't to be trusted."

"We can't stay here." Ceadda added.

Osfrid agreed. The group made their way deeper into the town. It was eerily quiet. Only the distant sound of laughter emanating from the taverns on the waterfront broke the silence. The Varangian called Velmud led them down an alley and into a small stone hut that they had taken over during the few days inside the town. The place must have been empty for a few years as the roof had caved in at some points and the wooden furniture had worn and rotted away. A pallet lay on the far wall; a broken table lay in the centre and a cracked stone fireplace dominated the back wall.

"We have to assume that Ragner has betrayed us." Acca seethed.

"If he has then I'll rip out his filthy innards." Hunweld growled.

Osfrid held up his hands.

"If he has betrayed us then surely we would have been captured at the gate." He turned to Hunweld. 'Ask your man whether they found Olaf."

Hunweld asked Velmud the question in Greek. They spoke for a few minutes.

"Aye, He says that the slave master lives in a hall next to the docks on the Western side of town."

For the first time in a long time Osfrid felt hope. He told his men to try and get some rest and to be ready to move out in the morning.

*

Early the next day, the two Varangian's who had been posing as the night watch on the Eastern gate buried the bodies of the men they had killed deep in the woods. Afterwards they made their way through the town, rendezvousing with Osfrid and the others. They spent a week scouting out the town, getting to know the layout of Olaf's hall, of its defences and manpower. Finally on the seventh day they were ready.

As the sun had risen rain clouds had swept in from the sea causing drizzle. The town's populace rose from their beds with the coming of the dawn. Fishing boats put out to sea on the morning tide and merchants set out their wares.

Osfrid and Hunweld set off across town towards Olaf's hall, the others following at a discreet distance, ready to act if trouble arose.

They had changed out of their armour and instead were wearing clothes similar to the natives, A cloak, worn over the tunic, fastened on both the breast and shoulder with the assistance of a brooch. Osfrid regretted not being able to take their shields, but the bulky things would have generated too much suspicion from the locals.

They made their way through the mud covered streets, the smell of rotting fish, urine and manure permeated the air, dogs barked and whined. A pig farmer shepherded his herd through the alley they were taking forcing the party to press their backs to the walls.

Finally they came to a clearing. It was an open square with large strong wooden houses enveloping three sides.

"The wealthy part of town." Hunweld whispered. Osfrid nodded in agreement. Each of the houses was similar in size to those of a wealthy Thegn's hall in England. He took in the sight, observing the presence of several tough looking men loitering nearby.

"Are they guards or Mercenaries, maybe?" Osfrid asked his father. Hunweld looked the men up quickly before turning back to his son.

"Mercenaries I reckon. See the mail under their leather jerkins, only a paid mercenary would be able to afford such armour, and I bet a man like this Olaf would want men he could trust."

Osfrid turned and looked back down into the alley they had emerged from. He waved the others to follow. Acca, Ceadda and the Varangian's made their way into the square. The loitering men looked at the group as they walked towards them.

"Easy now." Osfrid warned.

Hunweld whispered to his men in Greek. The Varangian's then quickened their pace. They spoke to the mercenaries in Nordic feigning friendship, putting them at ease.

They laughed and joked, the Saxons joining in pretending to know what was being said.

Without warning the three Varangian's quickly drew out their daggers, cutting down the mercenaries closest to them. The Saxons did likewise. Within moments the group of men were dead, their throats cut, or stabbed through the heart.

"Well that was easy." Acca smiled, cleaning his bloodied blade on his sleeve.

"That was too easy." Ceadda growled. The big man helped the Varangian's move the bodies.

They dumped the corpses in a latrine running down the side of the square. They then piled as much mud and excrement on top of them to conceal them before rejoining with Osfrid.

Hunweld pointed to the house on the left.

"This is Olaf's." He explained.

Velmud and his compatriots drew their axes, taking up positions on either side of the halls large wooden door. Osfrid drew his sword, and with a mighty kick smashed it open. He charged in, the others at his back. Inside they found themselves in an open space which served as a feasting hall. A long table dominated the centre of the room and over a dozen expensive looking chairs and Hunting trophies adorned the walls and a smoky fireplace was lit at the room's far end. It looked as though the hearth had just been lit meaning that if they were lucky Olaf could still be asleep. A terrified slave cowered in a corner.

Hunweld grabbed the young boy and shoved him roughly to Velmud. The Varangian asked the boy several questions in Nordic before dragging him outside and letting him go, setting him free.

"Olaf's quarters are further inside as are several guards."Hunweld explained, pointing to the narrow passage ahead of them. Velmud spoke again. Hunweld nodded.

"He says that the slaves are held in a shack on the far side of the compound overlooking the shore. We have to cross through a courtyard and through the entire hall before we can reach it."

Osfrid rolled his shoulders loosening the muscles.

"It looks like we will have to fight our way through." He said as he strode deeper into the hall.

The others followed, at his back with weapons drawn.

They moved quickly through the passages, surprisingly not seeing another soul. The earliness of the hour had proven to have been an advantage as Osfrid had hoped. A man like Olaf, who had a reputation for laziness and debauchery, was most likely still sleeping off the previous night's frivolity.

They came back into the sunlight after arriving in a spacious courtyard. Across the open space was the stone shack that housed the slaves. Upon seeing it, Osfrid broke into a run, Acca close on his heels. The others spread out to keep watch.

Osfrid reached the shack. A heavy oak door with an iron lock prevented access. He swore under his breath. If they tried to break it open with weapons then the noise would surely awaken the entire household and Olaf's guards. He spun around. A loud chuckling echoed across the courtyard.

"So you are Thegn Osfrid Hunweldsen" boomed a vicious voice. 'Finally you have come to free your family. How delightful." The voice mocked in heavily accented Anglisc.

Osfrid bounded back into the courtyard. He looked to his right and saw that his father had formed his men into a defensive position. They looked naked without their shields, exposed. He caught a look of alarm in Hunweld's expression, his father pointed to the halls roof, where to his horror a dozen archers were lined up. Their weapons trained on his men.

Standing in front of them was the obese figure of Olaf fork beard the dreaded slave master of the North Sea. He wore a shirt of mail that must have been altered considerably for it to fit over his grotesque body. Osfrid narrowed his eyes in fury. Standing next to the slave master was Ragner, an evil grin on his face.

"You Traitorous bastard." Acca shouted as he recognized the man.

Ragner laughed.

"I am no traitor. Olaf is my master. Always has been, I am a pirate and he hires us to capture slaves." The Viking pointed his sword at Osfrid. "You killed my friends, slaughtered them like animals. I will take great pleasure in seeing you die."

"You won't see a thing after I rip out your fucking eyes." Hunweld bellowed. Ragner laughed mockingly shaking his head in amusement.

Osfrid pointed his sword at the slave master.

"You and I have business. Where are my wife and daughter?"

His voice was quiet, threatening, hiding the fury that was growing inside of him. He had come so close, only to have his chance of saving his family torn away. No. He would get them back.

Osfrid took in his surroundings. The roof was six feet off the ground. With enough speed he might be able to jump and climb up to his foes. Surprise is what he needed. He glanced at Acca. The younger man looked back in understanding. Osfrid smiled humourlessly. Olaf was mocking Hunweld who had exploded in a fit of swearing and threats at his enemies, Distraction. Osfrid nodded to Acca.

With startling speed Acca drew back his arm and threw his sword high. The blade pirouetted through the air catching the archers by surprise.

Olaf and his men were slow to react.

Osfrid took his chance and sprinted forwards. He jumped and used his own sword as an anchor. Within moments all hell had broken loose.

The bowmen loosed their deadly arrows. One narrowly missed Osfrid's head as he hauled himself up onto the roof. Olaf and Ragner stepped back. Osfrid was amongst them in seconds. His dragon sword was like a blur as he slashed and cut his way through the archers. He was unaware of the screams, of the blood spraying him of the blade piercing flesh.

He was berserk, blood drunk, in that moment he knew what the gods must feel like. He felt invincible, fed by his despair, his anger, his fury he was unstoppable, and a god of combat. In moments it was all over. The dozen archers lay dead at his feet. Blood dripped from his sword, his clothes, everywhere.

Only Ragner and Olaf remained, the fat man cowering behind his young servant. Terror was etched on both of their faces.

Down in the courtyard Acca was helping Ceadda stand. The big man had been hit by an arrow in the knee. Two of the Varangian's lay dead riddled by arrows. Velmud knelt over the bodies of his comrades weeping silently. Hunweld clambered up onto the roof to stand by his son, murder was in his eyes, and it was fixed squarely on Ragner.

"Now,' Osfrid said calmly, unnerving his enemies even more. 'You will tell me where my wife is."

Olaf stuttered and began to fumble inside his shirt. He pulled out a large iron key. Osfrid smiled cruelly. Walking over to the slave master he took the key and threw the fat man from the roof. Olaf screamed. He crashed to the ground with a crunch, Osfrid jumping down after him. That left Hunweld on the roof with Ragner. Osfrid didn't see what his father did to the man as he made his way to the slave hut, but the scream the young Viking let out, made even him shudder.

*

The Iron Gate swung open with a creek that echoed throughout the stone structure. What had appeared on the surface to have been little more than a shack had turned out to be a large complex of dungeons and cells. Osfrid had his sword pressed into the slave masters back. Acca following close behind not prepared to let his master out of his sight.

Olaf led them through a series of turns, down a flight of stone steps and through a dark passageway. At the end of the passage was another heavy door. The sounds of the sea grew louder. They reached the cell door.

"Please spare me."Olaf whimpered.

Osfrid sneered at the man, he was a coward. A man who had built a reputation through fear and piracy, but who in fact had not been good at either. He dug his sword in harder.

"Open the door."

The slave master fumbled with the lock before the cell door creaked open, Osfrid almost wretched at the stench that wafted out of the cell. He forced the door open wider, covering his mouth and nose with his hand leaving Acca to guard the slaver.

Cautiously he stepped into the cell. It was dark, only a small barred window allowed light to come in. The sun was still low in the sky but enough light shone through to show the cell.

Lying in the corner on a pallet was a small figure. Only the long scraggy red hair identified her.

"Aerlene. My love" He whispered.

The figure didn't move. She was asleep. He knelt down next to her, brushing her hair away from her face. Despite the grime and lice her features were as beautiful as he remembered them to be. He kissed her softly on the cheek. She stirred, her eyes flickering open, for a moment there was no recognition in them only confusion and fear.

"I came for you my love." He said softly, stroking her hand.

Her eyes widened, she sat up and with a sob wrapped herself around him in a savage hug. Her cries came then, a deep sobbing that shook her emaciated frame. He could feel the tears running down her cheeks, he whispered soothingly into her ear. Apologizing for taking so long, for leaving her, they both wept.

For a long time they sat together in the stinking

cell holding each other tightly in silence. She felt so fragile; he feared that he could snap her in two. It wasn't long before his anger at the man responsible for her condition came to the surface. He gently untangled himself from her embrace and helped her to her feet. He scooped her up into his arms, surprised at how little she weighed and carried her like a small child out of the cell.

Acca stood as they came back out into the passageway. He hauled the slaver out before them. Once back into the courtyard he punched the fat man into the dirt.

Hunweld rushed to his daughter in law, taking her out of Osfrid's arms and into his own.

Osfrid turned to the slaver who was cowering in the dirt. Both Acca and Velmud stood over him there weapons digging into his stomach. Olaf whimpered.

"I have my wife. Now you will tell me where my daughter is." Osfrid said quietly. He crouched down next to Olaf and gripped his face in his hand forcing the fat man to look at him.

"I sold her." Olaf answered miserably.

"To who?" Osfrid asked.

"I sold her to the king's household. He likes to have pretty servant girls." Olaf stammered in his high pitched voice. Tears threatened to pour from his eyes as he saw the look of fury in Osfrid's face.

Osfrid punched savagely, rocking Olaf to the floor. Blood began to pour from the slavers nose.

"Handel took her to Bergen a week ago. It was too good a price to turn down." The slaver whimpered.

Osfrid drew his sword. He'd taken what he'd needed from the pathetic wretch cowering at his feet. With a quick movement he drew the blade across the slavers throat silencing the wretch with a pitiful scream.

The fat man's body crumpled into the dirt, blood pooling around it. Casually Osfrid wiped the swords blade on his robe before facing his companions.

"Our task is still not complete.' He said to them all. Ceadda was now standing, his leg bandaged by a piece of bloody cloth. Acca stood by Velmud who was helping Hunweld bury their dead in the courtyard. Aerlene was now standing, her features haunted and gaunt but defiant.

'My daughter is in Bergen enslaved in the house of King Hardrada. We must get her back. I know I am asking a lot from you. Freeing my wife from a slaver is one thing, but to go up against a king is quite another. I understand if you decide to head back to the ship but I am going after Esma. I'd rather not go alone."

Hunweld stepped forward. "The girl is my granddaughter. I would march into hell itself and spit in the devils face to get her back. I am with you, as are my men."

Acca was next. "I failed to protect your wife and daughter before; I will not do so again. I will go."

Osfrid thanked them both. Ceadda was about to speak but Osfrid stopped him.

"My old friend you are injured." He said.

Ceadda waved him away dismissingly. "It's but a scratch lord. I can fight as well as any of you buggers."

The others chuckled. Osfrid put his hands on his steward's shoulders.

"I need you to look after my wife. Take her back to the ship and protect her.' He faced them all. 'We make for the ship. Father and Velmud can use what gold we have left to hire some locals to help man the oars and navigate us to Bergen. When all is ready, we sail for Hardrada's castle."

***

22.

It took four days to reach Bergen. The winds were favourable and the knowledge of the three locals that Hunweld had hired had proven invaluable. In all that time Aerlene had not spoken another word, she had withdrawn into herself. She only ate and drank when Osfrid told her to. If he didn't then he was sure that she wouldn't. He had done his best to get through to her but was only met by a blank stare. His heart was breaking.

It was night as the ship slowly rounded an inlet, the moon was high and bright, lighting the way for their passage up a narrow river.

Hunweld was at the front of the ship with one of the natives he had hired from Oslo. The blonde haired Norwegian was holding a long pole which he used to test the depth of the river. When the water became too shallow he whispered to the oarsmen to slow. More than once the rowers had to use their oars to force the boat into deeper water.

Finally the boat rounded the curve of the river, and there before them was the port of Bergen. The shining moon gave Osfrid an unrestricted view of the harbour.

Hundreds of thatched houses spread out in all directions the smoke from their hearths rising lazily into the night air. He could see very little movement from the towns populace but the usual sound of taverns and whorehouses carried across the water. Already docked in the bay were dozens of fishing and merchant vessels but worryingly he caught sight of three large longboats.

"The king's here alright." Said Hunweld, moving to be with his son. He pointed to the largest of the anchored ships.

"Must be Harald's flagship, you see the banner flying from its mast." There flapping lazily in the wind was the banner of the raven, Hardrada's flag.

"If he's here than so is Esma." Osfrid replied his gloved hands gripping the rail tightly in anticipation.

"What's the plan son?" Hunweld asked.

During the four days it had taken them to reach the port Osfrid had been deep in thought. At first he had believed that they would have to take similar action to get Esma as they had done to get back his beloved wife, but now he was contemplating an entirely different strategy.

"Harald is a king. He has no quarrel with me and he is like you father, a man who served the Emperors of Constantinople for many years. I intend to simply ask him to give her back to us."

Hunweld stared at his son in disbelief for a moment before breaking into laughter.

"Ask him! The most ruthless man to have ever served as a Varangian and you plan to walk into his stronghold and ask him" He chuckled for a few moments before composing himself. He smiled at Osfrid. "God willing, it's so ridiculous that it might just work."

The Norwegian who was guiding the ship into dock spoke to Velmud.

"He says we should prepare to dock." Hunweld translated.

It took another hour of skilful sailing to bring the ship into port. They chose the western most dock as no other ships were tied up there. Osfrid didn't want to attract any unwanted attention.

*

They waited until dawn before disembarking the ship. Fishermen were already out at sea casting their nets and the angry squawks of seagulls filled the air. Osfrid sent Velmud and one of the other Varangian's ashore to scout out the castle that lay on top of a hill overlooking the port. Whilst they waited Ceadda prepared a meal for the men.

"How are you my love?" Osfrid asked his wife gently.

Aerlene was wrapped up in a heavy cloak and sat at the bow of the ship. Her red hair shone in the early morning sunlight. She hadn't spoken to him since their escape from Oslo; her eyes were distant as though she was looking at some place far away. He had spotted her shaking violently and more than once during the nights he had heard her calling out. He wrapped her up in his big arms and held her tight, kissing the top of her head softly.

He'd spent most of the voyage to Bergen washing her and cleaning away the lice that had infested her clothing and body. He had thrown her torn and filthy clothes into the sea, dressing her in a spare pair of clothes that had once belonged to one of the Saxon sailors. The breaches and shirt gave her a masculine appearance but she lost none of her attractiveness in the process.

He longed to hold her as they used too, to be intimate with her again. He felt shame when such lustful thoughts entered his mind. She had suffered terribly, guilt overrode the lust tenfold.

He spent many hours just talking to her, very rarely receiving an intelligent response. It felt as though the woman he had once loved had been chased away, dragged into some deep dark pit in her mind. He wondered if things would ever again be the same between them. Saving Esma would heal some wounds of that he was sure. But then what if a similar fate had befallen his only daughter? He wasn't sure if he could handle such a blow. No, he shook his head angrily at the thought. She would be safe, and he would bring both back to Driffield in one piece.

"My lord"

Osfrid looked up to see Acca walking over to them. The younger man handed him a bowl of soup.

"Thank you Acca."Osfrid thanked him. He stood up and handed Aerlene the bowl and spoon, he whispered in her ear and kissed her on the cheek before standing.

"How is lady Aerlene?" Acca enquired, falling into step with his lord. They walked to the docking ramp and stepped ashore.

Acca clapped his Lord on the back reassuringly.

"At least she is alive milord, which is what matters. My ma always used to say that time heals all wounds and it's true. Just look at me!" It was true. In only a few months Acca had come back from the near edge of death.

Osfrid couldn't help but smile at the younger mans eagerness.

"Well Acca I shall pray she will be like you, only not quite as ugly."

Acca laughed.

Osfrid turned to watch the bustling activity of the town; it always amazed him how similar everyone was. Every port in England would be doing virtually the same things. Fishermen would be heading out to sea; blacksmiths would be starting their day's labour and merchants would be selling their wares.

Later that afternoon Velmud and his companion returned from their scouting of the city. Osfrid and Hunweld met them on the quayside.

"What news lad?"Hunweld asked gruffly.

Velmud smiled at his captain and informed him of what they had learnt.

"Hardrada is definitely here, son. He asked one of the guardsmen and he confirmed it. The castle is busy preparing for a feast."

" A feast?" enquired Osfrid.

Velmud nodded and spoke to Hunweld. " Aye, he says the king is expecting an important guest in the next few days."

"Who?" Osfrid demanded.

Velmud looked at the two Saxons nervously before explaining;

"The guard said it was an important man from England, a man who was coming to discuss the matters of kingship."

The two Saxons looked at each other in confusion.

"Why would Harold send a man here? Could he be looking for allies perhaps?" Hunweld muttered. "Harald cannot be trusted. He sold out the Empire and betrayed the Varangian's to the Rus, all in the name of gold and wealth."

Osfrid frowned at the revelation. He wanted to simply go to the castle and beg the Norwegian king to free his daughter, but now with this intriguing news he knew that his goal would change. He was curious to know who the important Saxon was.

England was in turmoil at the death of Edward, enemies abounded from both outside and from within. In the months since he had left home anything could have happened. William of Normandy may already have invaded or perhaps Morcar and Edwin had caused more trouble in their quest for an independent Northumbria.

"I will go to the king as planned, but we must know who this English visitor is." Osfrid said adamantly. He waved to Acca and Velmud before facing his father once more.

"Look after Aerlene father. If we're not back by dawn tomorrow, take the ship and return to England."

Hunweld assured him that he would defend his daughter in law with his life. Acca and Velmud joined Osfrid on the quayside. Each man wore chainmail shirts covered by leather jerkins and cloaks. Velmud strapped his big war axe to his belt, the Varangian's favoured weapon of choice. Acca had long since replaced the old sword given to him by Ceadda. Now he carried a strong Viking sword taken from one of the Berserkers he had killed at sea. As usual Osfrid had his Dragon sword at his side. The golden hilt shone in the sunlight giving it an almost magical appearance.

The three companions said their farewells and headed towards the foreboding castle sat ominously on the hill overlooking the town.

It took them an hour to walk the distance, trying to pass through the town discreetly had proven difficult and only Velmud's mastery of the Norse language had avoided suspicions being raised. The road to the castle was busy with activity. Servants and merchants were rushing about their business in preparation for the upcoming feast.

The stone walls towered over them ominously as they approached the gate house. A burly looking guardsman blocked their path. He raised his hand telling them to halt. He carried a spear and wore mail emblazoned with Hardrada's emblem.

Velmud spoke with the man telling him who they were and their business. Osfrid hoped that the King would see him now that word had spread that a Saxon was due to arrive soon. After a few minutes of heated exchange the guard relented and barked at a young lad to fetch his captain. Dark clouds were rolling in from the East and rain threatened. The guardsmen told them to wait, and it was another hour of waiting in the cold rain before they were granted access to the castle. A tall slender man dressed in a leather jerkin met them as they entered.

"Greetings," much to Osfrid's surprise the man welcomed them in Anglisc. "My name is Haakon Hokinson I am the king's steward. I must ask you to relinquish your weapons."

Acca and Velmud hesitated a moment before Osfrid nodded that it was okay. He unbuckled his sword belt and handed it to the steward. The others handed their weapons over.

"Look after it." He growled.

The steward handed the weapons to one of the guards before gesturing for them to follow him. As they entered the castle a small group of armed guards fell into step with them. Osfrid glanced around hoping that he hadn't just walked into a trap. No, they would be fine; Hardrada had no quarrel with him. The main hall was dark and smoky from the dozens of candles that lit the way. It was surprisingly sparse of decoration only the heads of hunted beats adorned the walls.

Haakon noticed Osfrid's interest. "The king does not see the point of fancy decorations; he believes that his sheer presence is enough to impress his guests."He said airily.

"Such a belief must save him some coin." Osfrid replied sarcastically.

Acca walked alongside his lord. "What about Handel milord, the bastard could still be here. If he recognizes me from the beach skirmish we might all be killed." He whispered cautiously.

Osfrid nodded in agreement. The scum responsible for taking his family was more than likely still in the area.

"We'll cross that bridge when we come to it. I just want my daughter."

The steward led them into a drafty room and told them to wait until summoned. The room had a sturdy table with a selection of food and a stone jug of water.

The three men sat down and waited.

*

The steward knelt before his king. Sat on a cushioned throne was King Harald Hardrada, the most fearsome Viking warrior alive. His muscular frame gave him a formidable appearance but it was his face that struck fear into his enemies. His thick beard and savage face intimidated the hardiest of men.

The room was busy with servants hastily rushing about preparing the hall for the grand feast.

Harald waved at the man to rise.

"My lord king, our Saxon guest is waiting. What is your command?"

Harald turned to the man standing next to his throne.

"It seems we are having a lot of Saxon guests these days. Who is this Osfrid Hunweldsen?"

Handel stepped forward and bowed politely before answering carefully;

"The man is a Thegn milord, an enemy of my master Tostig. No doubt he has come here to disrupt the talks that are due to take place. Kill him sire and my lord will be most indebted to you."

Harald raised an eyebrow.

"How brave of him to come here in person, I have no quarrel with this man and I owe your master nothing." The king replied harshly.

"I would speak with him. "The king waved airily.

The steward bowed again before leaving the throne room.

"Sire, this man is dangerous, and err well wants me dead. Kill him... please." Handel pleaded.

The king laughed mockingly.

"From what I've seen of you I wouldn't blame him. The way you fuck my serving girls against their will shows just what sort of a man you are. Lucky for you I too am a bastard." The king laughed as he groped a young serving girl who had come to refill his cup of mead. The girl was silent as he fondled her breasts, terrified to defy her king.

"Selling girls into slavery too, what a heartless cur you are." He growled hungrily as he spotted his newest servant being yelled at by her master. "The Saxon bitch is indeed as beautiful as you promised. Very soon I shall see if she was worth the gold."

The girl was Esma.

*

Osfrid and the others stood before the king. Hardrada's laughter still echoed throughout the hall.

"You ask me to return to you your daughter! I paid a lot of gold for her Thegn Osfrid. And I've not sampled her delights yet." Laughed the king.

Osfrid could feel the rage building. "She was taken by my enemy, a wretch of a man. A man who rightly deserves the gallows for the crimes he has committed. You have no right to keep my child." He snarled.

"Watch your tone Thegn Osfrid. Your next words could be your last."Handel snapped. Osfrid turned his gaze onto the man who had ripped his family apart, the man who had raped his wife. Handel flinched under that relentless stare.

"I promise you that it will be my sword that pierces that black heart of yours." Osfrid threatened.

Hardrada laughed.

"You entertain me Thegn Osfrid. I am not a heartless man and you have claim to your daughter. I have a proposition for you." Harald said as he stood. Osfrid almost took a step backwards. The man was huge! Osfrid was tall but the king before him was a whole head taller.

"What do you propose?"

A grin crossed the king's features.

"I will return to you your daughter in exchange for you staying here as a gift to my guest."

Handel smiled wickedly.

"Guest? Who is your guest?" Osfrid asked as a knot of dread entered his gut.

Harald smiled savagely. "A man you have had many dealings with I believe. Tostig Godwinson. He will be arriving shortly to discuss the throne of England."

Osfrid swore under his breath. He should have known the mysterious guest was Tostig. Who else would come here? The realization of what the King had just said sunk in.

"He wants you to join his cause against his brother." Osfrid stated dumbfounded. He had no idea that Tostig would be willing to side with a Viking for the sake of vengeance.

Harald laughed; "but vengeance is not all. I want the crown of your kingdom. Britain, once more in the hands of the Norsemen, A noble cause don't you agree my Nordic brother?" he said staring at Velmud, who shifted uncomfortably under the Kings staring eyes.

Osfrid was tempted to spit in the Kings face at the revelation, but doing so would only get them all killed, as would his refusal. He noticed the heavily armed warriors that had entered into the chamber. Each wore mail and was armed with an axe or sword.

"Milord, you can't." Warned Acca as he sensed that his master was about to give in to the king.

Osfrid faced him, gripped his arm and pulled him into an embrace.

"You have been loyal Acca." He lowered his voice to a whisper. "Get the men from the ship and come for me; we won't let Tostig leave this place alive."

He released Acca and faced Harald once more.

"Very well, I accept your terms lord king. My friends are to be allowed to leave with my daughter?"

Harald scowled, the thought of losing his pretty slave irritated him. "Very well'; he finally replied after a long silence. 'They may go. Return their weapons as they leave."

The steward bowed and ushered Acca and Velmud out of the hall. Esma was escorted into the hall confusion on her pretty features. She saw Osfrid and ran to him. She hugged him fiercely.

"Father." She sobbed, "thank god you came, but I can't let you sacrifice yourself for me!"

Osfrid untangled himself and looked into his daughters teary eyes.

"You must go my child; this is the only way to get you home safe. I have your mother; she will be overjoyed to see you." He said hoarse with emotion.

The steward returned and led Esma out of the chamber, her cries fading as she went.

"Well lord king you kept your word, and so shall I." Osfrid growled.

***

23.

Out in the towns harbour a ship sailed into port. The sails flapped lazily in the wind, they bore no insignia, just a white sheet pulling the boat onward.

Ceadda watched from the quayside as the men onboard skilfully brought their vessel to berth. A small crowd of townsfolk hurried to the ship, calling out to the men onboard no doubt trying to sell their wares or the whores to sell their bodies. He leaned casually against a fisherman's shack doing his best to appear inconspicuous.

He took a bite of the apple he'd bought from a market stall and looked to the far end of the port where his own ship was docked. He knew that Hunweld would be watching the newcomer with interest. He frowned as a dozen armed men disembarked; each looked savage with the swagger of mercenaries.

Finally a smaller framed man disembarked his reddish hair glinting in the afternoon sunshine. The man wore a fine outfit of dark velvet and wore deerskin boots, about his neck was a gold amulet. Ceadda slowly made his way through the gathering crowd to get a closer look. He reached the ship and slipped in amongst the traders vying for attention.

The townsfolk could see that the red haired man was wealthy and they crowded about him seeking coin. The mercenaries roughly shoved their way through the crowd making way for their master. Ceadda listened to the words of the mercenaries as they threatened and swore at the crowd. He was surprised to recognize the language of Flanders.

He had worked with a Frisian long ago, before he'd joined Hunweld's estate. He had to make a double take as he heard a name being called. One of the mercenaries was in frantic talks with the wealthy looking man. Ceadda's heart tightened he'd heard right. The man was Tostig! He slipped out of the crowd and made his way back to Hunweld and the others. With Tostig in the town they were all in danger. It was time for them to leave.

*

Osfrid was thrown to the ground before his enemy. A bemused look was on Tostig's wretched face as he knelt down and looked his foe in the eye.

"Well, well, well, if it isn't my old friend Osfrid. I am so glad to see you." He sneered.

Osfrid spat at him causing one of Tostig's men to violently strike him with a gauntleted fist. Osfrid felt his nose break and his senses spin. He collapsed to the stone floor of Harald's castle. The Viking king roared with laughter.

"I am glad to see you are pleased with your gift earl Tostig. But I am more interested to see just what you have brought me." The king said greedily.

Tostig turned away from Osfrid who now lay unconscious, a puddle of blood pooling out from his damaged face.
Tostig faced the king and spread his arms wide.

"I offer you a kingdom my lord king."

A gasp came from Harald's courtiers who filled the chamber. The king himself coughed in feigned surprise before rising from his throne.

"And just what kingdom do you speak of?" he asked in anticipation.

Tostig smiled. "Why, my brothers of course, the richest prize in Christendom. England."

*

Hunweld and his men approached Harald's castle. The day was long over and the blackness of night had covered the land. Ceadda had reported the news of Tostig's arrival and shortly afterwards Acca and Velmud had returned with Esma.

The girl was safe on the ship; two of his men were guarding her. They were so close to having his family back together again and now it was Osfrid's turn to be rescued. Hunweld had ordered his men to pad their boots with cloth to muffle their movements. He'd ordered them to use charcoal to cover their faces until only the whites of their eyes could be seen in the gloom. Each of them wore their full panoply of war, heavy chainmail and helmets.

The Varangian's were all masters of guerrilla warfare trained to strike at an enemy where they least expected it. His thoughts drifted back to the Byzantine invasion of

Sicily. For days he and his men had hidden in the ruins of a church only to emerge in the middle of the night to launch raids against their Saracen enemies. They were like demons coming from the dark as they descended upon the terrified Muslims, their mighty war axes glinting in the moonlight as they went about their grisly work. Now here he was again, launching a night raid against impossible odds with only a handful of men. They lay in a ditch under the castles western wall, all they could do was wait for Velmud and Acca. He'd sent the two of them in the front gate, a risky move but one he was confident the young men could pull off.

He could see a guard patrolling the wall, flaming torch in his hand and spear in the other. The guard looked into the courtyard of the castle, the sounds from within distracting him. Hunweld had planned the rescue to coincide with the great feast that was now well under way. He hoped most of the town's garrison would be too drunk on mead to offer a strong resistance.

The sound of a door opening caught the guard's attention, then the hushed voice of a man in distress. The guard dropped his spear and raised his hands in surrender. Hunweld smiled, the lads had done it. A whistle came from the wall. The Varangian's silently stood and dashed to the base of the fortifications. A rope slithered over the side of the wall. One after the other the Varangian's scaled the rope. Hunweld took the rear and hauled himself over the wall to find Acca holding the castles steward at knifepoint and Velmud taking the guards weapons.

"Good work lads." He said clapping Acca on the shoulder. "Now we have to find Osfrid.' He grabbed the steward by the hair, 'and you my friend are going to take us to him."

The terrified man nodded quickly, he stared wide eyed at the group of fearsome warriors. Acca smiled and prodded the steward with his dagger.

"Let's be off then." He whispered in the man's ear.

*

Quickly and quietly they made their way through the winding passages of the castle. Hunweld was pleased to see that he was right. Most of the guards were drunk or too busy chasing the serving girls to notice the armed men stealthily moving through the castle. Those that did were quickly and quietly dispatched, their bodies dumped in empty rooms as they went.

The steward led them to a staircase that led down into the castles dungeon. He told them that the jailor on duty would have the key for Osfrid's cell. Acca thanked the helpful man before rending him unconscious with a sharp blow to the head with his daggers hilt. Hunweld and three of his men took the lead and entered the dungeon catching the jailor by surprise. The young man had been happily drinking himself into a coma before their arrival, he slurred at them and vainly tried to draw his sword but his drink addled brain instead caused him to collapse to the floor.

Hunweld chuckled before leaning down and taking the now drooling jailors keys from his belt. He ordered Acca to dump the steward and jailor into a cell which he then locked behind them.

“Osfrid” called Hunweld into the dungeons darkness.

“I’m over here. Took you long enough.” Acca grabbed a torch from the wall and walked to the voice. Sure enough there was Osfrid chained to the wall his face a bloody mess.

Hunweld chucked the keys to Acca who then tried each one on the cells door. “You look awful.” He joked as he worked. Finally with a click the door swung open. He tried the keys on the chain at Osfrid’s wrist but to no avail.

“Hold on lord I’ll get you out.” He said, drawing his sword.

Osfrid’s eyes grew wide; “You’d best not bloody miss, lad.” He said worriedly. Acca smiled and swung the blade with all of his strength. The chain snapped upon impact freeing Osfrid from the wall. Acca held out his hand and hauled his lord onto his feet. Osfrid thanked him and hugged his father.

“Here;’ his father said passing him a bundle; ‘get dressed and let’s get the devils arse out of here.”

Osfrid quickly donned the leather jerkin and boots the Varangian’s had smuggled in with them. He was pleased to see they had managed to retrieve his sword and gratefully kissed the blade.

“Time to kill Tostig.” He snarled.

Hunweld shook his head.

"Don't be a fool; we would never get past all of Hardrada's men. We have to leave before it's too late."

Osfrid bit his lip in frustration before reluctantly following his fathers lead.

They made their way back out of the dungeon and the cell that housed the unconscious jailor and steward and up the stone steps. Velmud led the way, he halted them with a raised hand, and someone was coming. Every man pressed themselves against the narrow corridors wall hoping that they would not be noticed in the darkness. The footsteps grew louder, whoever it was, was carrying a torch to light their way. There was more than one person; Osfrid could make out the footfalls of a group of men. He tightened his grip on his sword, they would surely be discovered.

The footsteps stopped before carrying on and then fading once again. Whoever it had been was now heading away from them.

Every man sighed in relief.

They set off once more heading back to the wall they entered by. The sounds of the feast carried on interrupted; no one had noticed their infiltration. One by one the Varangian's and Saxons abseiled back over and down the wall before disappearing into the night like wraiths.

Part Three

BATTLES

24.

July 1066

Driffield

Osfrid was happy despite the troubling news that passed throughout the kingdom. For the first time in years he had his entire family with him. He smiled as he watched Esma chase her younger brother across the fields of long grass, now in bloom with a dazzling variety of flowers. Birds sang and the sun shone and for now at least the world was as it should be.

The return journey from Norway had taken several weeks but thanks to the skilled Norse sailors he had hired in Oslo they had reached home safely. As a thank you he gave the ship to them and a bag of gold. Before they set off back home they had thanked him, promising to send word if Tostig or Harald set sail for England. He smiled to himself at the fury Tostig must have felt at discovering he had escaped his clutches.

As soon as they reached Driffield he had dispatched riders to Harold who was preparing his army in the south. News had reached them that William of Normandy had amassed a huge fleet and was biding his time to cross the channel. War was inevitable it was just a question now of who would strike first, the Viking or the Norman.

He laid his head back on the grass and faced his wife who was snoring softly. A hint of sadness on her face, a look that he feared would never leave her. Gently he stroked her cheek and chuckled as she smiled and opened her eyes. He kissed her on the forehead.

"I am sorry." She whispered.

Osfrid held her hand.

"You have nothing to be sorry for my love." He replied kindly.

She sobbed and hugged him fiercely. He held her as she finally told him of her torment at the hands of Olaf and Handel. When she was finished he held her tightly and swore to her that Handel would see hell soon enough.

The sound of hooves made him look back across the fields. His father and the Varangian's were returning from York. The city was now under the command of Morcar and his brother, both men had profited greatly from their rebellion against Tostig but dark rumours were circulating that they intended for Northumbria to become independent. The riders rode up the hill into Driffield but Hunweld trotted his horse over to Osfrid and Aerlene who still held onto Osfrid tightly.

"The sniffling little toad." Hunweld growled as he dismounted his horse. He held the reigns and stood next to his son.

"What's Morcar done now?" Osfrid asked tiredly. Just for once he would like to leave the kingdoms troubles alone.

"He refuses to send men south to join up with the king. He claims that he hasn't the men to spare with Tostig on the rampage and his threat of invasion."

The previous month Tostig's mercenaries had raided the coast and even made landfall and attacked at Sandwich on the south coast. Harold had marched against them and easily defeated them but it was clear that Tostig was getting bolder.

"If the Vikings do come then they will land in the North father." Osfrid pointed out.

Hunweld snorted derisively. "I'd wager a Saxon housecarl against a Viking Berserker any day. It's the Normans that are the true danger. Morcar wants to keep his men here to weaken Harold."

Osfrid gave his father a hard look.

"You really think Morcar wants Harold to lose?"

Hunweld spat in disgust; "Aye I do, Morcar wants his own kingdom, his family always has. Maybe the silly fool thinks that William will split the kingdom with him."

Osfrid stood and patted the grass from his tunic. He held out his hand and helped his wife up from the soft ground.

"Have you any news from Cearl?" he asked.

Hunweld smiled, "Aye I have. Morcar has given him lands not far to the south of here; I also heard that he'd been made Marshall of the North."

Osfrid raised his eyebrows in surprise. "Cearl is to command the northern army? In that case I should go and see if he needs any help."

*

Acca was sweating as he swung the axe. The summer heat had caused him to shed his tunic, his bare broad chest heaved as he chopped the wood before him. The village's blacksmith needed plenty of wood to keep their forges aglow and today it was Acca's turn to do the strenuous task. His muscles rippled as he raised the heavy axe high and brought it down savagely. The thick block of wood splintered neatly in two causing him to make a satisfied grunt. He placed the axe next to the chopping block and leant down to pick up his water flask, greedily he gulped down the water within.

"Someone's thirsty."

Acca coughed in surprise causing him to choke and forcing him to spit the water out onto the grass. Laughter came from behind him. He turned to find Esma giggling. Her long hair shone in the sunlight and her eyes glittered mischievously. Acca felt himself blushing and quickly grabbed his tunic and held it in front of him.

" Aw I was enjoying the view." She pouted.

Acca snorted. "I bet you were, my lady." He replied sheepishly.

Esma brushed a strand of hair behind her ear and walked slowly over to him. Her hips swayed seductively and her dress revealed her legs as she moved.

"I wanted to thank you Acca." She said softly standing close to him. "You risked your life trying to save me and my family." She placed a hand on his chest and slipped it down to the scar where the Viking spear had stabbed him. Acca couldn't breathe; this beautiful young woman was intoxicating. She smelt like flowers and her skin was a flawless bronze from the summer's sunshine. She looked him in the eyes, and without saying a word kissed him softly on the lips.

He kissed her back unable to resist her. Since the first time he had laid eyes on her all those months ago he hadn't been able to get her out of his mind. He knew they shouldn't be doing this; Osfrid would no doubt kill him if he caught them. He broke the kiss and held her at arm's length. He caught his breath.

"We can't my lady. You are my lord's daughter; you are meant for a noble not someone like me." He reasoned.

Esma stood back away from him. Hurt in her eyes.

"From the moment I saw you I loved you." She whispered; 'my brave warrior the man who saved me."

She took his hand and held it tightly.

"Tell me you do not love me too. I've seen the way you look at me."

Acca looked away, torn between his lust and his loyalty to his lord. He had dreamed of this moment for months, he hoped his desires hadn't been too obvious to the others.

Esma pressed on; "My father wants me to be happy. You are a good man Acca; no man is more loyal and kind."

She pulled him gently into her embrace and kissed him softly. "I don't want to marry some old Thegn; I want someone kind and young."

Acca looked into her eyes. His heart was torn. He knew that now they were back in England Osfrid would start to look for suitable husbands for Esma and he wasn't sure he could stand it if she was wed to another.

"If your father finds out...' he muttered as she kissed him again, deeply and passionately. Guilt flooded his mind and roughly he pushed her away. His breathing was ragged.

"We can't do this Esma. I cannot betray your fathers trust." Angrily he put on his tunic and strode away.

Esma stared after him.

***

25.

Dover

Harold stood on the high cliffs the sea breeze causing his cape to flutter out behind him. He stared out across the dark blue of the channel and narrowed his eyes. Barely visible on the horizon was the land of Normandy. A land that now threatened his reign like no other. His spies reported in regularly that the Dukes invasion plan was nearing completion; soon he would come and try to take England. Harold was confident that he could weather the storm. He had raised the Fyrd and now at his command were thousands of fighting men. Most were farmers pressed into service but the sheer number he had raised would be enough to drive his enemies back into the sea.

At his army's core were the Housecarls, fearsome warriors that were more than a match for any Norman Knight. He had heard concern from his generals about the Normans use of cavalry; they feared the beasts would ride straight over the Saxons. At this Harold had laughed. No beast or man could ride through the unbreakable shield wall. Harold unfurled the scroll that he held in his hands and read the latest reports from his earls. He frowned as he saw that his brother had landed a sizeable force at Sandwich. Luckily his earls had driven him back into the sea. Tostig was becoming more and more of a problem. One that he was sure would challenge him directly sooner or later.

*

Osfrid arrived at Cearl's estate in the late afternoon. Acca and Ceadda accompanied him. Each of them enjoyed the ride through the Yorkshire countryside, revelling in the Suns comforting heat. Song birds flitted to and fro in their quest to catch the multitude of insects that swarmed along the hedgerows and amongst the fields. None of them wore armour, just loose fitting tunics and breeches but each of them wore their swords. Cearl's new home was built from strong timber and was larger than the hall at Driffield. They could see a small group of men on top of the roof relaying the thatch. Cearl was stood on the ground looking up at them and giving instructions to his serfs.

The man had aged considerably since Osfrid had last seen him. The trauma of losing his wife and children at the hands of Tostig's cronies had taken away of much of his vitality. His hair was now cut short and a dull grey but his features were the same.

Osfrid raised an arm and hailed his friend; Cearl turned and shielded his eyes from the bright sunlight with his hand. Upon recognising his visitors he laughed with happiness.

"Osfrid, My friend is that you?" he called; he walked towards the riders his arms open wide.

Osfrid stopped his horse and dismounted. The men embraced like long lost brothers.

"It is good to see you my friend." Osfrid said jovially. Ceadda and Acca also dismounted, Acca took the reins of Osfrid's horse.

"Come inside out of this heat, you all must be thirsty." Cearl bellowed across the yard at one of his servants to take the horses to be fed and watered. A small skinny man jogged over to them and took the horses reigns and led the beasts to a nearby stream.

Cearl chatted and laughed with them all as he led them down a lane behind the roofless hall.

"I'm taking you to one of my out houses, the last winter's storms rotted the big hall that you saw as you came in, and this place had been abandoned for years, before Morcar gave the land to me." He explained as they walked.

"How so?" enquired Ceadda as he looked around, the place seemed familiar to him. They came out of the lane into a spacious open yard. At one end stood a stone cottage with a small wooden shed in the long grass. The memory returned to him as he took in the sight.

"This land once belonged to a wealthy clergyman. A bishop I believe. When Tostig began his reign of tyranny the bishop was exiled from the North and all of his possessions confiscated. Must have been about six years ago that it happened."Cearl explained.

"Cynesige was his name if I recall." He added as he led the way inside the stone cottage. Ceadda smiled at the name that was how he recognized the place. He had been sent here one winter to help the Bishops men hunt a wolf that had been feeding off of his cattle. The man had been a jolly plump man who was generous with his ale and food.

Cearl asked his guests to sit and make themselves comfortable. He ordered a serving girl to fetch them some fruit and drink. "The orchard on the south hill produces some of the best apples I've ever tasted." He said cheerfully.

Osfrid smiled; glad to see his friend apparently happy after the horrors he had suffered.

"So, my friends what brings you to see me? I trust your little adventure in Norway proved successful?"Cearl asked, taking a seat and ruffling the ears of an old dog that was lying on the cottages reed floor.

"I came to see how you were doing. And it seems you are doing very well indeed."Osfrid replied.

The serving girl returned and placed a bowl of juicy looking apples onto a table. She poured the men a cup of water each, before curtsying politely and leaving.

"Morcar was very generous to me after what happened... "His voice trailed off sadly.

Acca and Ceadda glanced at Osfrid, who nodded knowingly. He placed a hand on Cearl's arm and squeezed it reassuringly.

"I promise you Cearl, we will have vengeance. And as for Norway I encountered our mutual enemy there."

Cearl looked at Osfrid in disbelief.

"Tostig is in Norway, whatever for?"

Osfrid leant back in his seat and crossed his arms.

"He was there to try and convince the Norsemen to attack England.

I do not know if Hardrada agreed to do it but before we left the two of them seemed to be getting along rather well. I fear it will be the North that shall see war before the South."

Cearl stood and paced the room, His face a mixture of emotions.

"Does the king know of this?" he asked.

Osfrid nodded. "I sent word to him as soon as we arrived back home."

"And yet he does not send troops North" Cearl exclaimed disbelievingly.

"That is why I have come to see you; I hear that Morcar has made you his Marshall. You must tell him to prepare for an invasion. Harold will not dare leave the south coast unless absolutely necessary." Osfrid explained.

Cearl halted his pacing and looked at Osfrid with a helpless expression.

"Morcar and Edwin will not listen to me Osfrid. They gave me this land and that title to keep me busy and out of their plans. I may be a Marshall but only of the few men here." He waved his arm despairingly.

Osfrid glared at his friend sternly.

"Tell me Cearl. Is Morcar planning to betray Harold?"

Cearl couldn't meet that stare and looked at the floor.

"Harold came to see Morcar whilst you were away, he does not trust Morcar but he was convinced enough that the North would stay loyal. I however don't think that Morcar will, but he will not do it openly. Not until..."

"Until he knows who the victor of this mess will be." Osfrid finished for his friend.

*

Osfrid and his companions left Cearl's lands in the early evening and slowly made their way back to Driffield. Osfrid had convinced Cearl to try and appeal to Morcar to reign in his ambitions at least until England was safe. He knew it would be futile but hoped it might buy them some time to warn Harold of the rising threat from within.

"I do not envy Harold one bit." Ceadda had said as they had mounted their horses. Neither did Osfrid. It was bad enough that the kingdom was under threat from the Normans but now Harold would have to contend with challenges from Norway and from his own earls. And then of course there was the hatred from his brother.

Many men would have conceded defeat against such odds but not Harold, and for that he had earned Osfrid's deepest respect.

The light was beginning to fade as they crossed the stream that led to the hill up to Driffield and stars were beginning to shine in the warm night. A cool breeze blew in from across the sea, from the direction of Norway.

Very soon the hammer would fall; Osfrid wondered where it would strike the hardest.

26.

South Coast of England

August 1066

The days slipped by one by one and yet the enemies of the Saxons still did not appear on the horizon. The Fyrd was becoming restless and men deserted daily to return to their families and crops. Harold had gambled that Normandy would strike first and in his gut he knew that William was simply biding his time.

No doubt Norman spies were sending him the news that the Saxon army was slowly weakening. Every day he had ridden to the coast to ensure his men were being vigilant and every day he was met with the same replies from his bored men. It was the 28th of the month and soon the summer would begin to give way to the autumn. It was still hot and the sun baked the kingdom, the fields were full of unpicked crops and wheat. Every day he was told by his advisors that the harvest must be collected before the bountiful crops spoiled.

With a reluctant heart he had been forced to disband several hundred of his Fyrd and allow them to go back to their homes. What was worse was that the Witan had warned that the legality of keeping the kingdoms Fyrd in the field was due to expire. If they did not attack soon then Harold would have no choice but to disband thousands of troops or risk rebellion.

His brother Gyrth believed that the core of the army would be more than enough to repel an invasion. Harold too had confidence in his Huscarl's but like any other general preferred the advantage of greater numbers.

He had established camps all along the south coast, his strategies had been made and yet his enemy still did not come. He prayed to god to give him the strength to best his foes.

*

Orkney Islands

The small boy ran along the sandy beach laughing and playing with his friends. Excitement was in the air as the men of the islands had begun preparing for war. The flag of King Hardrada fluttered from the wooden ramparts overlooking the shore and it was here that the group of boys played. The boy slowed and came to a halt. He squinted against the bright sun that was riding high in the clear blue sky. He shouted in excitement. There on the horizon he could see the distant shapes of hundreds of ships. The king had come at last and now the Norsemen would go to war.

It wasn't until the early evening that the ships anchored off the shore. Ships packed with burly Vikings, horses and supplies were spread all along the islands coast. The islands inhabitants came out of their homes to greet them and to pay fealty to their king. The boy stared wide eyed at the thousands of warriors. Campsites were set up wherever there was a spare patch of ground; soon the air stank of hundreds of fires and the smell of cooking meat.

The boy ran back to his father's hall, it was the largest on the islands. His father was the jarl and would be the person the king would visit first. He ran through the crowds of men only to find the hall guarded by some fearsome looking warriors. He sighed in disappointment; no children would be allowed entry now. He looked around and spotted his mother and the villages other women all rushing about trying to provide food and ale for the Viking lords. A thought occurred to him. He rushed around the side of the hall and limbered himself up. He often snuck out of the hall at night and used the same way to get back in. He climbed up the side wall of the hall; the walls were thick with moss which he used to clamber up. He hauled his small frame up and spotted the narrow gap that separated the thatched roof to the wooden frame. He breathed in and squeezed and wriggled his way inside. He edged his way deeper inside until he could see and hear the men gathered within.

The main hall was full of the most powerful men of the Norse lands. Sat at the head of a long table was the King. His massive frame looked awkward in the chair in which he sat. Next to him on his right hand was Tostig. Other men of note were the jarls of the Shetlands, Iceland and men from Ireland. The chatter faded away as the King stood and lifted his horn of mead into the air.

"My brothers of the axe and the shield, I welcome you here." He bellowed, a rapturous cheer filled the hall, "We are here after a long voyage, the finest warriors of the Norsemen are gathered and eager for war!." Another cheer broke out. "This night we shall discuss the next phase of our campaign to take the throne away from the snivelling Saxons."

Tostig frowned in annoyance at those words but quickly covered his displeasure with a false smile.

The king took Tostig's hand and made him stand.

"This is the brother of Harold Godwinson, a man who knows how treacherous a man the false king can be. He will be my advisor during our war."

Shouts of greeting and a few of derision at having a Saxon in so prominent a position responded.

A young Viking named Eystein Ori stood. The man was in his early twenties but he had a fearsome reputation as a warrior and was quickly becoming one of the king's favourites. The king had even offered his beloved daughters hand in marriage to the man.

"My lord king, perhaps our Saxon ally can tell us what we should expect when we land in England." Eystein asked confidently.

The king waved for Tostig to stand which he did hesitantly. Tostig had known this time would come; finally his dream of vengeance was coming to fruition, now he had to make the Norsemen believe that the people of the North would back them and more importantly him rather the usurper Morcar.

He cleared his throat. "We can expect support from the local populace in the North. We may even find allies to aid us, the hatred of the west Saxons still lingers even after a century. The north still has strong links with the Norsemen of Denmark and of your selves." There were snorts of scorn at the mention of the Danes.

"Our first target should be York as from there we will be able to consolidate our position and supplies before marching South into the heart of the Kingdom."

Harald nodded in agreement.

"What of the man who usurped you Earl Tostig, this Morcar? Will he resist?" Eystein Ori demanded to know.

Tostig turned his gaze onto the younger man and stared at him venomously.

"The man is a coward, if he resists he will die."

***

27.

17th September 1066

York

The news had spread like wildfire throughout the northern lands. The town of Scarborough had been sacked, and all of it's inhabitants enslaved or put to the sword. The Norsemen were on the move, first they had sailed down the coast of Scotland ravaging as they went. All forces sent to oppose them were routed or annihilated. An army sent by Morcar was soundly defeated at Holderness and refugees were pouring south to safety. Tales of Norse brutality instilled fear in all who heard them. Hardrada marched with his banner 'the land Ravager' before him.

The city of York was in an uproar as the unstoppable march of the Vikings grew ever closer.

Morcar's fleet had been outmanoeuvred on the river Ouse and now Norse ships were being spotted in rivers and estuaries all across the region, even at Driffield the warning beacon had been lit for the first time in a generation. Osfrid had rallied his Fyrd to defend the village but no attack had come. It had been a tense few days and nights. When an attack was obviously not going to occur he had ridden hard for York where Morcar had called a war council of the Northern Thanes. He had left Ceadda and Acca as well as a contingent of his best fighters as well as the remaining Varangian's to protect his family.

Hunweld and Velmud had gone with him to York.

They arrived in the city in the early afternoon; the place was swarming with armed men. To Osfrid it seemed as though Morcar and his brother were raising an army. They made their way through the dusty streets towards the city's main Hall. The sun was still scorching hot and the heat magnified the stench of a bustling city. Supplies of grain and water were being stockpiled; blacksmith forges were busy making weapons and armour. The war that had been threatening for so long was now upon them.

They entered the hall and found the place in an uproar. Thegns were arguing with one another, many feared for their lands worried that Morcar would leave them to suffer at the hands of Hardrada's army. Sat at a long oak table on a raised platform at the back of the hall sat Morcar. His features were heavy with worry. He slouched in his seat with his head in his hands. Osfrid pushed his way through the noblemen, catching sight of Cearl and Edwin in the process. The two men waved wearily to him.

"The devil's tits what the hell is the fool doing?" Hunweld growled, angry at the pathetic site of the man who should have been rallying his men.

Osfrid mounted the platform. "Fellow Thegns of the North hear me!" he bellowed raising his arms so that all could see him. The bickering stopped and the hall went silent.

"We must not allow fear to overcome us, we must prepare for war against Hardrada's army.' He turned to face Morcar. 'Earl Morcar, it was here just short of a year ago that we marched with you against the tyrant Tostig. Take heart in this and know that we will march for you again against this greater enemy."

Morcar stirred as though being shaken from a daze at those words. The hall echoed with shouts of agreement with Osfrid.

Osfrid stood before Morcar and offered the man his hand. After a pause Morcar smiled and grasped it.

He walked to stand in front of the table.

"My brother Saxons, Thegn Osfrid is right. We must fight the Norsemen. Despite our defeat at Holderness we must try again. I loathe engaging them in open battle, but it is in battle, with you all behind me that we can best them."

A great cheer filled the hall in response.

"Gather your men, we march in three days."

The hall quickly emptied as the Thegns rushed to prepare their men for battle leaving Osfrid and Hunweld alone with Morcar, his brother and, Cearl.

"I'm glad to see you Osfrid" greeted Edwin.

"News from the North has been grim indeed. I fear that engaging Harald in battle could be a mistake, I was there at Holderness, and it was a slaughter.' Edwin gave his brother a hard stare; 'I had too few men."

Morcar laughed. “Next time we will fight them and beat them. The North can stand alone.”

Tensions had been growing between the two brothers since the sack of Scarborough and now it was clear that Morcar had underestimated the threat he was faced with.

“Has any word been sent to the king?” Osfrid asked the men before him.

Morcar scoffed and waved his hands dismissively.

“This is a problem for the North; it is none of Godwinson’s concern. And besides he would never reach here in time.”

Osfrid slammed his hands onto the table in frustration startling the others.

“Enough of this foolishness, your desire for an independent North will be the death of us all!”

Edwin placed a hand on Osfrid’s shoulder in warning.

“Calm yourself friend, my brother is still your earl. “He whispered.

Morcar glared at Osfrid. Anger was in his dark eyes. Hunweld tensed, his hand hovering above his sword hilt.

"Gather your men Osfrid and bring them to York. I will deal with you after we have defeated the Norsemen." Morcar spoke quietly and threateningly.

He gestured for Edwin and Cearl to follow him as he left the hall.

Hunweld stood next to his son and chuckled.

"You certainly have a way with people son. C'mon let's get back home and raise the Fyrd. We have a battle to fight."

***

28.

20th September

Fulford gate

Half a mile from the city of York, at Fulford gate Morcar's and Edwin's army formed ranks ready to fight the approaching forces of the most fearsome warrior of the Viking world.

On the right flank was the river Ouse, its waters flowing serenely in the hot afternoon. Dragonflies darted above its surface and midges gathered in swarms in the Suns heat. On the left flank was marshy ground known as the ford lands. The ground there was muddy and deceptive. It was here that Osfrid and his men had been stationed. He did not doubt it was a punishment for his words in York. He had brought over a hundred men from Driffield and its surrounding area. Most of the men were only basically trained. Most wore leather jerkins embossed with iron for armour. Only the Huscarl's would wear the expensive chainmail.

Five thousand Saxons stood in a long line waiting for the arrival of the Norsemen. Scouts had reported that they were approaching rapidly. Harald had split his army into three and soon each portion would converge upon the waiting Saxons.

Osfrid wore his full panoply of war. His helmet with the face guard was polished to a glaring shine. Aerlene had painstakingly cleaned and prepared his chainmail until it too shone in the hot day's sun. On his left arm he carried a heavy round wooden shield plainly decorated. In his right hand he held his sword. The golden dragon emblazoned on the hilt drew envious glances from the warriors around him.

He glanced to his left and smiled at Ceadda. The big man wore full armour as well, except he carried his mighty axe rather than a sword. At his belt he had a short stabbing sword that would be useful when the shield walls joined as one in the dance of death.

Standing to his right was Acca. The young man too wore an expensive set of mail that Hunweld had made for him. He looked nervous but took strength from knowing he was surrounded by his friends and countrymen. Further down the line were Hunweld and the Varangian's.

Osfrid felt sorry for the Norsemen who would face those men in combat.

Every man was sweating under the baking sun; the ground was dry and hard causing dust to swirl in the wind.

Osfrid tried to see Morcar over the heads of his men but could only see Cearl. Anger tightened his gut, no doubt Morcar and Edwin would be at the army's rear, ready to bolt at the first sign of trouble. Osfrid had learnt that despite the men's bravado, they were both cowardly and self serving. He knew the only reason Morcar had ordered the army to engage the Norsemen was to take the credit for their defeat and to show the Northern nobles they didn't need the King or the South.

Excitement rippled down the line as a great dust cloud was spotted in the distance quickly approaching. A few moments later the sound of thousands of marching armoured men reached their ears. It was the sound of thunder rhythmically ringing out across the plain. Ealdred the bishop of York, and his priests walked up and down the Saxon lines invoking prayers and blessings upon the warriors. Ceadda knelt before the Bishop for his blessing as did many other men. Many crossed themselves or muttered silent prayers, either to Christ or to the old gods. Osfrid knelt and scooped up a handful of dirt. He let it fall through his fingers and prayed for the safety of his friends and his family. He didn't believe in any one god but prayed to any that would listen.

A horseman galloped out of a copse of trees and towards the army. It was a Saxon scout. "They come, prepare for battle!" the man shouted before rearing his horse to a halt and leaping from the saddle. He ran into the ranks of men and took up his position in the shield wall.

The thundering footsteps grew louder and sure enough emerging onto the ground before them were the Norsemen. At the head of the army rode Harald Hardrada and next to him also on horseback was Tostig Godwinson.

Osfrid roared a challenge, but was drowned out by the noise made by five thousand men also hurling insults.

The Saxons banged their swords onto their shields making a deafening racket. The rhythm of the banging increased as more of the Norsemen came into view. Quickly the Vikings formed ranks and roared their own challenge at the Saxons. Their shields locked together creating a seemingly impenetrable barrier.

"Advance!" bellowed Morcar from the rear ranks. Osfrid saw what the earl intended. The Norsemen were still forming ranks and reinforcements were arriving all the time. Now was the time to strike, he just hoped the Norsemen didn't have too many reinforcements.

With a roar the Saxons jogged the first few feet towards the enemy before breaking into an all out charge. The right flank smashed into the Vikings taking them by surprise. A few seconds later Osfrid on the left was slamming into his foes.

The initial charge broke the Norsemen's unready shield wall allowing the Saxons to hack and slash their way deep into the enemy ranks. Osfrid cut down a Viking berserker slicing his blade into the man's neck. Blood sprayed covering his face and hand. He parried an axe blow with his shield and thrust again feeling the blade sink deep into flesh and glance off of bone.

Screams filled the air as the Saxons carried all before them. Osfrid staggered as a sword struck his helmet almost knocking him off of his feet. Acca leapt over him and sent the Viking attacker crashing to the floor with a hit from his shield.

With a savage downward thrust Acca drove his sword deep into the man's guts. The stench of shit and blood permeated the air. Men were falling all around them. Osfrid shook his dazed head, and glanced around him. He could see the right flank was collapsing as more and more Norsemen reinforced the river side of the battle. He clambered to his feet and yelled for Acca and his men to form a shield wall. Soon they would be surrounded unless they could hold their ground.

Ceadda swung his axe decapitating a berserker before he launched himself at another enemy. The man parried the blow with his shield staggering Ceadda and was about to slash his own axe at the big man, when Acca again came to the rescue. He caught the deadly blow on the tip of his sword and brought his elbow savagely into the Vikings face causing him to crumple to the ground.

Osfrid raised his shield and barked orders for his men to form up on him. Within moments a hundred men had locked their shields. The wall was formed and began pushing back against the Norsemen's savage counter attack. Osfrid cut down three more men before he noticed that the right flank was on the verge of collapse, and they would be engulfed by the enemy. He swore, Morcar had ordered the charge too soon. The Saxons were close to exhaustion and yet more and more fresh Norsemen were entering the fray.

The left flank was being forced into the boggy ground of the ford lands. The footing was becoming treacherous as the heavy fighting had churned the already marshy ground into thick mud. Men were falling into the mud and being trampled by the advancing Norsemen. Osfrid and his men fought desperately but it was no use. Harald had reinforced his centre and now the entire Saxon line was close to buckling.

Osfrid watched as Harald Hardrada himself and his bodyguards charged into the fray. Being carried for the king was his royal standard the Land-Ravager as before him scores of Saxons fell. Fighting was fiercest near the river. Osfrid caught a glimpse of Hunweld and the Varangian's. Even they were being driven back by the onslaught.

Acca yelled a warning. Osfrid spun to look to the left and could see another force of Norsemen marching through the trees beyond the ford lands. Once those men arrived on the scene then they would be completely surrounded and only death would greet them.

"Fall back to the city!" he roared to his men. The same call was taken up by the men in the centre, he watched as Edwin and Morcar fled to their horses and bolted back to York.

"Bloody cowards" yelled the men as they saw their Earl's flee.

The Norsemen launched another push and this time the Saxon line broke. The Vikings swarmed through the breach cutting down Saxons without mercy.

Osfrid turned and fled along with the others leaving behind a trail of blood soaked earth and broken bodies. Escaping the Norse pincer movement many of the Saxons fled into the ford lands, where they floundered in the boggy ground until cut down or sucked into the quicksand's, on the right flank most drowned as they fell into the Ouse, once a serene river, now a place of unspeakable horror. Soon the marsh and ditches were clogged with the bodies of English dead. The Norsemen waded in blood marching over the impacted bodies as though the marsh was solid ground.

It was a dark day for England but hope was not lost.

***

29.

Driffield

Aerlene looked at herself in the small ornate mirror her father in law had brought with him from the East. The frame was intricately decorated in swirls and spirals of gold leaf. To someone in England it would be worth a small fortune.

She frowned slightly at the face she saw before her. Once she had been young and fresh faced, her green eyes had shone with mischievousness. But now she feared that was lost forever, taken by a monster.

Handel.

His hideous face flashed into her mind causing her to cry out in fear. The things he had done to her..., "Osfrid must never know". She whispered into the empty room. It shamed her that she couldn't have fought the wretch off. She slumped down onto the bed on which she sat and sobbed.

A voice in her mind chided her for being so weak; another praised her for doing what was necessary to protect her daughter from harm. She felt as though she was losing her wits altogether. She had gone to the village's chapel everyday to pray to God for his forgiveness, his understanding, but all of her pleas had fallen on deaf ears. She was in despair. Her husband had done what he could to make her feel loved and safe, but he was an important man who had many other worries, and problems to deal with.

She felt guilty at distracting him from those matters. She knew that she had been cold to him, had been difficult to be with. She wanted more than anything to go back to the way she was before the nightmare of her captivity. She drifted into a troubled sleep and dreamt of her husband and the good times they had shared before the world had turned into hell.

She awoke to the sound of her son's laughter. She sat up groggily and made her way outside into the courtyard. There her son was playing with his sister. Esma was tickling his face with a feather and holding the wriggling boy down. Aerlene could not help but smile at her children. They were worth living for. A sense of peace filled her as she watched them play. All she had endured was worth it to spare Esma the horrors she would have surely faced at Handel and Olaf's hands. Wulf looked up and saw his mother. He called out to her for help from his sister. Esma stood back and let her sibling run away and into his mother's arms.

"How long will papa and, the others be gone for mama?" the little boy asked.

Aerlene hugged her son doing her best not to show the fear she felt for her husband and friends. Hunweld had always been kind to her and Ceadda was already considered a member of the family. She had even grown fond of Acca; despite the looks he often gave Esma. Aerlene had noticed the two's blossoming friendship in the months since they had returned from Norway and knew her daughter wanted more from the young man than just friendship, despite her best efforts to hide it.

"They will be back soon." Esma said as she noticed the tears welling up in her mother's eyes.

"They're busy fighting Vikings?" Wulf asked.

"Yes, and they will beat them." Esma replied confidently.

Esma was about to ask her mother if she was alright when a boy from the village ran into the courtyard, his small podgy face red from his running.

"My lady! My father sent me to tell you that ships have been sighted off the coast."

Esma noticed her mother's gaze go distant, like it did so often these days. She had to take charge.

"Mother." She said sharply snapping Aerlene out of the daze she had slipped into.

Immediately she focused her attention on the little boy who was only a year or two older than Wulf.

"You're the blacksmiths boy aren't you?" she asked. The nobility inside her took charge.

"Yes, milady Aefre is my name. Father was worried that they may be Viking ships."

Dread knotted itself inside her. With all of the able bodied men away in York the village would be defenceless against any attack. Osfrid had left a handful of spearmen to protect them but against a determined Norse raid they would be of little use. Her mind raced. If she ordered the villagers to flee to York they may end up running into the Norsemen's main army. They couldn't go North and to the South was a large tract of difficult terrain that woman and children would find hard to traverse. She remembered what her husband had told her about the hall.

"Run back to the village and tell everyone to come here, we have the palisades to protect us." The little boy nodded earnestly before turning around and sprinted back down the hill towards the village.

Aerlene hurried to the palisade and shouted for the spearmen to assemble. Hastily the six men gathered their weapons and leather armour. One of them climbed the watchtower and scanned the coast.

"My Lady, the boy was right. I see a handful of longboats beached on the shingle.' He raised an arm to shield his eyes from the suns glare. 'My lady, armed men are approaching, I can see more than a dozen." The spearman's voice trembled as he spoke.

Within the hour the villages inhabitants had arrived behind the palisades and the strong oak gates were bolted. The few men among them were elderly or too young, but they armed themselves with whatever was to hand. Small axes, kitchen knives, farming implements and hammers were their weapons. The women and children huddled inside the hall.

Aerlene stood on the palisade and wept as she saw smoke begin to rise from the village below. Rapidly it thickened and flames could be see flicking upwards above the trees. She prayed to god for protection and wished that her husband was there to protect them all. She took solace in knowing that no one in the village was being killed, homes could be rebuilt, and lives could not. She flinched as she heard the harsh tones of Norsemen approaching. Their voices carried on the smoke filled air.

They emerged from the copse of trees on the opposite bank of the little stream that led to the hill that housed Osfrid's hall. They wore armour and carried swords and axes. The uneducated spearmen had miscounted. There were at least forty of them. Feral grins on many of their faces as they sensed the easy prey and plunder behind the palisade. She could have held the place with a few more spearmen but their numbers were too many. A knot of fear wormed its way into her gut. She should have tried to flee; now they were trapped with nowhere to go.

"Lady Aerlene..." called a voice from amongst the Norsemen. She froze as she recognised it. She peeked over the palisade and saw the man who had raped her. Handel stood at the front of the warriors. He wore a coat of leather and a cap on his bald head. He smiled cruelly as he spotted her on the wall.

"Ah there you are my pretty. I hope your daughter is with you, I've yet to rut her like the little whore she no doubt is."

His men laughed, many calling out lewd remarks.

"My lord Tostig hoped your husband would be here, but alas it seems he has trotted off to war like the good Thegn he is."

Aerlene could barely stand, her breathing was ragged, and she was having a panic attack. Esma saw her mother slump against the palisade and ran to her side. Tears streamed down her face as she looked at her daughter.

"Forgive me, I have doomed us all." She wept. Esma hugged her mother tightly and whispered soothingly into her ear.

"You have nothing to be forgiven for mother. If that bastard lays a hand on you I swear I will kill him. There is a way out, trust me."

Esma called for one of the men to take her mother inside the hall before she turned and strode to the walls edge to see Handel. She was not afraid, she would not be afraid.

Handel smiled wickedly upon seeing her on the wall.

"Ah there she is lads, the wench that promises pleasure, every one of you lads will have a chance to fuck her, after I've had my turn that is." He laughed and his men bellowed with vicious glee.

He raised his arm signalling for a group of his men to move forwards. They carried a heavy log capped with a head of iron.

"It won't be long now, little whore. We will bash our way in and kill you all." He cackled.

Esma ran down the steps and into the courtyard. She yelled at the men to brace the gate. She ran into the hall and headed for the halls small armoury. The armoury was mostly empty thanks to the Fyrd taking the weapons and armour off to war.

She grabbed a short blunted sword from the wall mounted rack and hurried outside to find her brother staring at the gate. She watched the gate buckle; the men defending it threw their weight against the wood. Handel's men sang an almost cheerful sounding song as they went about their dreadful business, they sang of the rape and pillage to come. The gate began to splinter, the sound of its hinges squeaking and the cracking of the wood drowned out the singing.

Esma screamed as the gate broke open; the force of the ram's final impact sent several of the men bracing it flying backwards. Handel's men swarmed through the breach, their swords and axes swinging with wild abandon. The old men and boys were no match for their savagery. Within moments most of the defenders were slain causing Esma to flee back inside the hall. Only the few spearmen put up any form of resistance. She glanced behind her as she ran, and saw the attackers slaughtering the men who still stood to oppose them. A spearman cut down one of the attackers but was in turn dispatched by an axe blow.

Inside, the village's women and children were cowering. Esma called out for her brother, and found him huddled in a corner with their mother.

"We have to flee, Wulf get mother up." She spoke calmly to the terrified boy.

Wulf took his mother's hand and tried to help her stand. She would not budge. A vacant look was on his mothers face. She was in shock.

Esma shouted for the villagers to head for the palisades rear. Behind one of the halls out houses was a loose piece of palisade that led to a hidden path that led through the woods at the bottom of the hill. Only she and her brother knew of it. They used to sneak out and play amongst the trees or run away when their father was cross at them. Quickly Esma ran over to her mother, and forcefully hauled her to her feet.

"Run to the back fence Wulf, show the others the way into the woods. Go!" she cried.

The boy didn't hesitate; he nodded determinedly and called for the others to follow. Esma threw one of her mother's arms over her shoulder and made for the halls exit. They emerged into a scene of utter chaos.

Handel's men had swarmed in through the gate and into the courtyard. Many of them were setting fire to the outhouses causing smoke to blind the frightened women and children as they tried to flee.

Esma caught sight of her brother running towards the back fence; the little boy dodged the grasp of one of the attackers, kicking him square in the groin. She would have laughed if not for the chaos surrounding her. She lost sight of him in the smoke and headed in the same direction. She noticed that some of the spearmen and male villagers had not all been killed in the initial attack, she saw desperate fighting near the gate. She thanked god for them, those men had bought them the time they had needed to flee the now burning hall.

Tears streamed down her face as she watched her home burn to ashes around her. Her mother stared at the chaos around them. Esma wept for her also. Her mother was lost to her, her mind broken from the horrors she had endured during their captivity.

She made her way through the courtyard, past the dying, struggling figures whirled amongst the smoke and flames.

She blindly helped her mother towards freedom, they were so close. Just as she dared hope that they had escaped a pair of strong hands grabbed her by the hair and hauled her down roughly onto the hard ground. She lost her grip on her mother as she fell. Aerlene too sprawled to the ground and lay unmoving.

"Mother!" Esma cried.

The pain forgotten she scrambled to her mother. She never made it. Handel emerged from the smoke and kicked her hard in the stomach as she crawled, she curled into the pain. The sword fell from her grip, she was at his mercy.

"I've waited a long time for this you little bitch."Handel cackled wickedly. He shoved her onto her back with his foot. He unhitched his breeches and forcefully slid her dress over her thighs. She screamed and struggled against him. The bastard would take her, right there, right now.

She could feel and smell his foul breath on her, she punched and clawed at his face but he violently batted her hands away and pinned her down.

Just as he was about to force his way into her she felt his weight ease and heard him scream in pain. She opened her eyes and saw her mother standing over him; a rock was in her hand. Handel fell off of Esma, he held a hand to his head, it came away bloody.

"YOU BITCH." He yelled. He pulled a dagger from his boot and lunged at Aerlene. Esma screamed a warning, but it was too late.

Her eyes widened as the blade pierced deep into her mother's side, savagely Handel twisted the blade causing Aerlene to cry out in agony, and blood gushed from the wound. She collapsed to the ground, unmoving her eyes wide in terror.

"Now it's your turn." Handel growled as he turned back to Esma who lay stunned at his feet.

Weakly the girl called out for her mother, who lay lifeless only a few feet away. This time she did not resist, despair and loss filled her soul.

"Leave her alone."

Esma turned her head and saw her little brother staring at her and Handel. In his hands was the sword she had dropped. Handel sneered at the boy.

"The whelp, wait your turn boy, I'll gut you just like I did your mother." He mocked dismissively.

Handel turned his attention back to Esma, she cried out to her brother to run away, but the little boy did not.

"I said, LEAVE HER ALONE!"

With a high pitched battle cry Wulf ran at Handel and swung the sword with all of his strength.

The dull blade struck Handel in the side of the head knocking him once more off of Esma. Esma scrambled to her feet and ran to her brother.

Handel swore viciously getting to his feet. Blood poured from the wounds in his head. He drew his dagger again and marched threateningly upon the siblings. Esma turned to flee but Wulf stood his ground. Determination was on his young face.

The boy drew back the sword nimbly dodging Handel's dagger thrust.

The boys speed took Handel by surprise; he had no chance to react as Wulf thrust the sword at his face. The blunted blade pierced Handel's left eye, blood and gore sprayed from the now destroyed organ. Handel roared in pain collapsing to the ground, the dagger fell from his grip as he clamped his hands over the wound writhing in agonizing pain.

Wulf stood over him and raised the blade. He stared hard into the eye of the man who had just murdered his mother. Handel stared back.

"I swear...Boy...I will find you and I will kill you, you, and your bitch sister." The wretch spat.

Esma gently placed an arm on the boys shoulder. She spat at Handel and kicked him savagely.

Handel screamed for his men.

"We have to run brother, while we still have a chance."

Handel screamed for his men, the sound of running boots drew nearer.

The fighting had ended; Handel's men had killed the few defenders, and were now moving from building to building. Only the smoke hid the boy and his sister from their gaze.

Wulf took his sisters hand, and together they fled.

Their home was gone forever, and so was their mother.

30.

Woods, South of York

The remnants of Morcar's army had fled before the might of Hardrada's forces. Many had followed their lord back to York, but Osfrid had taken his men south, deep into the dales, and away from the city. It would only be a matter of time before the Norse army was at its walls, and sieges were not the Saxons forte. Osfrid walked through the trees, taking in the sight of his countrymen cowering amongst the trees.

His head ached; his hair was matted with blood from the axe blow that had knocked him senseless during the battle. The moans and screams of the wounded sent a shiver up his spine. No more than a hundred men had followed his lead into the countryside, which meant the bulk of the surviving shattered army would be trapped in York.

He walked until he reached the little stream that flowed through a small glade; gratefully he cupped his hands and drank the sweet water. He cleaned his wounds and washed his face, the cold water reviving his battered body. He turned when he heard approaching footsteps. It was Acca. The young man had saved his life and had proven he was a formidable warrior in his own right.

"Milord, are you alright?" the young man asked as he too splashed his face with the sweet water.

"It's just a scratch Acca.' Osfrid replied assuring his friend. He paused before walking over and gripping Acca's hand. "Thank you for saving me."

Acca smiled.

"If you keep this up lad, then I might just replace Ceadda with you, the man is getting old after all." He joked.

"Who are you calling old? You cheeky shit."Ceadda laughed as he joined them in the glade. The big man was covered in cuts and his thigh was wrapped tightly with a bandage of linen from where an axe had dug itself into his armour.

"You look awful old man." Acca mocked. Despite the horror at Fulford gate Osfrid could not help but smile at his comrades.

Even when their kingdom was on the brink of annihilation the men still laughed and joked.

Ceadda cuffed Acca round the head causing the young man to fall into the stream, soaking him from head to toe.

The big man roared with laughter. His laughter ended when Hunweld and Velmud entered the glade. Osfrid's father appeared to not have suffered a scratch. His armour was clean and no dents could be seen, his sword on the other hand would have to be sharpened. Several of the other survivors told of how Hunweld and his foreign friends had cut a swath through the Norse ranks before Hardrada himself had overwhelmed them.

Hunweld nodded to them as he sombrely drank from the stream. Velmud stood at his captain's side staring into the gently flowing water.

"There are only four of my men left alive." Hunweld growled.

The news shocked them all.

"Father, I am sorry." Osfrid offered his condolences. The Varangian's that had travelled to England had been his father's pride and joy. Each man had been a deadly warrior, skilled in warfare like no other men he had met.

"They died holding back the Norsemen. They are the reason any of us are still alive." Hunweld spat onto the grass. "It won't be long before the Norsemen take York and then the North will be lost."

Osfrid placed a hand reassuringly on his father's shoulder.

"Harold will come. He has to."

Hunweld nodded not convinced.

"Aye, he will come, and we will drive those bastard Vikings back into the sea."

*

The next day Osfrid led his small band of warriors west towards the old Roman road. He hoped that if Harold was coming they would meet him there. They kept to the woodland as they went. Smoke from dozens of burning villages and towns could be seen on the horizon. The few

Saxon villagers they encountered told them that the Norsemen had besieged York and that Morcar was negotiating its surrender. It came as no surprise that the opportunistic Earl would surrender so quickly, but the news from the south was a surprise. Rumours were spreading that the King was on his way North with a huge army at his back. They didn't know whether the Normans had landed or not, the army being spoken about could have been Williams.

Osfrid and his father both believed that Harold would come eventually regardless. They decided to head to the town of Tadcaster to wait. It took another day to reach the small town, moving through enemy territory had forced them to move carefully and slowly. They had seen several Norse patrols as they went. More news reached them as they settled into the town. Tostig Godwinson was rallying support for the Norsemen from the Northumbrian lords. Many still hated the West Saxons, wanting independence from their southern brothers.

Osfrid was sharpening his sword with a whet stone when news of Driffield reached the town. A number of refugees had managed to reach Tadcaster and were relieved to find their Thegn was still alive.

"What of my wife and children?" he asked of the middle aged woman standing before him. A little girl stood beside her and buried her face into her mother's skirts.

The woman wiped tears from her eyes.

"Lady Aerlene... I saw her fall." She sobbed.

'A man attacked your daughter as they were running, lady Aerlene tried to stop him, she was stabbed and she...she fell."

Osfrid stared hard at the woman, desperately trying to find some deceit behind her words, he found nothing but sorrow. A sorrow that now threatened to overwhelm him.

"My children?" he whispered.

The woman shook her head, wiping away tears.

"I do not know my lord. They saved us, showed us the way to escape. I think they got away." She said trying to ease her lord's pain.

Hunweld placed a hand on his sons shoulder and hugged him fiercely. Osfrid sobbed into his father's embrace. His comrades stood staring in silent despair. Each of them had loved Aerlene, had risked their lives to save her, and now she was gone, snuffed out from the world like a candle at the coming of the dawn.

The pain Osfrid felt was like none he had ever felt before, it was his mother's death magnified by a thousand. Hunweld whispered reassuringly into his son's ear.

"Be strong lad. Be strong for your people, for your children."

The mention of his children brought him out of his despair. His father was right. He needed to ensure his children were safe before he could mourn his beloved wife.

He looked around the room and waved at Ceadda to come over to him. The big man walked over, he still bore a slight limp from where the arrow had struck in Norway.

"My lord?" he asked cautiously.

Osfrid placed a hand on his old friends shoulder and looked him hard in the eye.

"I need you to find my children Ceadda. I would give anything to go myself, but I must fulfil my duty as Thegn and lead these people. There are sure to be many battles ahead my old friend, so promise me that you will find them and keep them safe." Osfrid's voice was hoarse from emotion as he spoke.

Ceadda gently placed a hand on his young master's arm and nodded.

"I will find them lord or die in the trying. I promise."

31.

Osfrid stared into his mug of ale, his thoughts tormented by his children and wife.

That morning he had ridden to Driffield with Acca and Ceadda only to find his home a scorched ruin. They encountered no Norsemen but evidence of their movements was all around. Columns of smoke to the north and the refugees that fled across the countryside meant that they were not far away.

Bodies of the dead were scattered all around shrouded in soot and blood. Most were the brave men who had brought the survivor's time to flee but some were women and children. They had spent much of the day picking their way through the debris, retrieving bodies and piling them in a group at the centre of what had been Osfrid's home.

It hadn't been until late in the afternoon that he had discovered the body of Aerlene. He had collapsed at her side and wept for over an hour, the others leaving their lord to his grief. He had screamed in anger to the heavens, blaspheming the god that she had loved so much, demanding to know why she had not been protected. His pleas and anger went unanswered. The world was on the brink of an abyss and God had abandoned them.

Rage threatened to overwhelm him.

After a time Ceadda had come to him and hugged the man he had known for decades. Finally they carried the lady Aerlene's body down the hill and into a grove not far from the ruins of the hall. A small pond surrounded by oak trees, it had always been her favourite place.

She had often come there to pray and think and it had been there that Osfrid had proposed marriage to her.

Acca and Ceadda had dug a deep hole and gently wrapped the body in cloth they had retrieved from the ruins. They buried her at the ponds edge and placed a rock on the site. Osfrid knelt by the grave for a time vowing to avenge her death.

He drew a knife and slid the blade across his left hand. He squeezed his hand into a fist and dripped the blood onto the stone. It was an oath forged in blood and no other oath was more sacred.

Finally they had set fire to the corpses of the villagers; to bury them all would have taken days, a luxury they could not afford. The sun was setting by the time they had finished their grisly task, the flames of the pyre flicking high into the sky. Osfrid and Acca said their farewells to Ceadda. The big man hugged them both fiercely promising he would return with Osfrid's children.

*

Now Osfrid was back in Tadcaster drowning his sorrows in the local tavern. He downed his ale and slammed the jug onto the table, causing a bang that spooked the already nervous patrons.

"So, here you are lad."

Osfrid turned bleary eyed to see his father standing behind him. Hunweld took the mug and gave it to one of the taverns serving wenches.

"How much have you had?" he asked

"Not enough" Osfrid replied drunkenly.

Hunweld looked at his son, seeing a broken man. It reminded him of him-self many years previously when his own wife had died in childbirth.

Hunweld sat at the table next to his son and ordered them both more ale.

Osfrid glanced at his father in surprise.

Hunweld smiled sadly.

"I know how you feel son, let's drink ourselves into oblivion and mourn our losses now, so that tomorrow we can be free of loss, and full of rage."

The two men sat in silence whilst they drank. The taverns patrons were oblivious to the men's loss. After a while Hunweld placed his ale onto the table and spoke softly; "I have something I must tell you son."

Osfrid looked up from the mug he'd been staring into.

"I guess I am asking for your forgiveness. In the east, In Constantinople I met someone."

Osfrid lowered his mug slowly placing it on the table."What do you mean?"He asked slowly.

Hunweld coughed nervously, unable to meet his son's eyes. "I met a woman..."

"A woman?" Osfrid said sitting up in his seat and giving his father a bemused look.

"Her name is Theodora. She is a Greek...and my wife."Hunweld mumbled.

Osfrid spat out the ale he'd been sipping, his father had said the last thing so quietly he'd almost not heard him.

"Wife! You have a wife." He slammed his mug onto the table splashing some of the ale onto the table. A sense of anger and disappointment raced through him. For the past ten years Osfrid had believed his father had fled to the East to mourn his beloved wife, Osfrid's mother. Now the sot was telling him he had a wife, a foreign wife.

"What about mother, did she mean so little to you." Osfrid growled feeling betrayed.

"Watch your tongue lad. I know you have been through a lot but never doubt my love for your mother." Hunweld replied angrily.

Osfrid stared into his mug of ale for a moment before chugging its contents. He gestured to the barkeep for another.

After ten tense minutes of silence Hunweld broke the stalemate.

"She saved me son." He said quietly. 'After your mother passed I was a broken man, I defied my king in my rage and almost cost us everything. I fled east to avoid people's pity, to try and find peace."

Osfrid sipped from his mug, leaning back against the stone wall. He had never heard the real reason why his father had gone. For years he had believed his father had fled because of his opposition to King Edward's pro Norman policies.

"I arrived in Constantinople. I never intended to stay there for long; I had hoped to move on to the Holy land, to Jerusalem and seek answers from God."

Osfrid raised an eyebrow in surprise. He didn't know that his father was a religious man. He remained silent waiting for Hunweld to resume his tale.

"I was in the city for a week searching for a guide to take me there. The Saracens had conquered their way deep into

Anatolia and passage further east via the sea was impossible; their ships were raiding and pillaging all along the coast. I thought that I had found someone, a grizzled old Greek by the name of Esterphos but before we started out the city went mad."

Hunweld stared at the wall as memories filled his mind.

"The emperor was losing support from the people, unknown to me I had arrived in a city on the verge of civil war. Mobs loyal to the emperor roamed the streets killing any foreigners they could find.

A group of the bastards found me, I killed six of them but more of the shits arrived on the scene. I was close to being surrounded, I was hurt, one of the buggers buried a dagger in my thigh and I was bleeding heavily and was getting weaker by the second. Just as they were going to tear me apart like an animal Theodora appeared." Hunweld smiled as the vision of her entered his mind. Osfrid scowled and finished his third mug of ale.

He ordered another.

"Why are you telling me all this? Why did you not say anything sooner?" he asked as the bar wench filled his mug.

Hunweld sighed sadly. "I tell you this son because now I see in you what was in me after your mother died. The pain will consume you if you let it."

Osfrid slowly lowered his mug onto the table's wooden surface and stared hard into his father's eyes.

"Good. I want the pain. I want to feel it when I bury my blade into Tostig's wretched heart; I want to feel it when I send Handel screaming to the deepest pit of Hell."

***

32.

September 24th 1066

Tadcaster

Word spread like wildfire of a vast army approaching the town from the South. The towns Thegn ordered his warriors to gather on the palisades and prepare for battle. No-one knew whose army it was; news from the South had been sparse and confused. Fears that the army could be Norman disappeared later that morning when an out-rider arrived at the towns gates. The army was Harold's.

The King had come to save the North from the Norsemen. The people cheered and orders were quickly given to prepare for the kings arrival. Food was prepared to feed the horde of warriors that was rapidly approaching. Acca stood on the palisade and looked south. The sight he saw took his breath away. Ten thousand Saxon warriors dressed in the full panoply of war and all on horseback rode up the old Roman road. Their spears glinting in the bright morning sunshine gave them a mystical appearance. He shielded his eyes against the suns light; there at the front of the vast column was King Harold. At his side rode his brother Gyrth and dozens of other nobles.

It was the largest army he had ever seen, and the speed of its march would go down in legend.

*

The arrival of the king sent a buzz of excitement through the town. Tents and campfires were rapidly set up as the vast army settled in to rest for the night. If a Norse scout was in the area they would of have to have been blind to not notice the columns of smoke drifting lazily skyward. Harold had made his way to the towns Thegn and demanded the latest news. Osfrid and his men crowded the hall and waited as Thegn Edgar informed the king of the battle at Fulford.

"Morcar is a fool." The king spat. Murmurs of agreement came from the gathered men.

Harold faced his subjects; he looked the epitome of kingship in his armour and long dark green cloak. His features however gave away the strain that he must surely be under. His handsome features were gaunt, and dark rings of weariness were under his eyes.

Osfrid too was tired. He and his father had not slept until the early hours of the morning having spent the night drinking away their sorrows. His head ached and the feint smell of vomit permeated from his beard.

"The army shall rest here this eve. Tomorrow we march on York, prepare your troops." Harold declared before dismissing the gathered men.

Osfrid walked outside and winced against the suns glare, the alcohol fuelled pain in his head stabbed into his brain like a knife. He was about to head to the nearby stream that passed by the town to clean himself up when his name was called.

"Thegn Osfrid?" it was the king.

Osfrid swayed slightly and rubbed his eyes in a vain attempt to stifle the pain in his head.

"Milord" he managed to reply.

Harold smirked slightly. "I see you survived Fulford. I am glad."

Osfrid nodded. "Thank you sire.."

"Clean yourself up lord Osfrid, and meet me in my tent this evening for the war council. I will need men I can trust if I am to win the day against our foes." Said Harold before walking away accompanied by his bodyguards.

The King strode down the road towards the town gate, Osfrid vomited into a nearby bush.

*

By the evening Osfrid had sobered up and washed himself. He wore a clean tunic given to him by Thegn Edgar, and Acca had polished his chainmail. The local blacksmith had replaced the links that had been damaged at Fulford and had hammered the dents and nicks out of his helmet and sword.

He fingered the dragon swords hilt marveling at the blade, it looked brand new and sharp enough to cut stone. He swore an oath that it would soon be cutting its way through Tostig and Handel's hearts.

***

33.

September 25th, 1066

York

The morning was bright, clear and hot. Harold had roused the army at the crack of dawn and by 6am the entire force had departed from Tadcaster. The Saxon warriors mounted their horses and set off to face the Norsemen, they were heading for York.

Osfrid rode a mount but his men had to march the distance as not enough spare horses could be found for the new recruits from the town and the surrounding villages. All night long the Kings scouts had ridden across the length and breadth of Yorkshire summoning all able bodied men to fight for their king. A few dozen men had arrived during the night but by morning over three hundred had taken up the call to arms. It was these men that Osfrid now commanded.

The journey only took three hours, no enemy forces had been sighted the entire time much to the amazement of the Saxons. Some leaders would have hesitated at the lack of any opposition, fearing a trap, but not Harold. He was confident in his martial abilities and so were his men.

They arrived at York in the mid morning, the Suns heat beating down upon them. Every man sweated under their armour and licked their lips with thirst. To Harold's amazement the city gates were thrown open, not a single Norseman in sight.

The king summoned Osfrid and a number of other Thegns to join him as he entered his city in triumph. The rest of the army stopped outside the walls, most went looking for a drink and a bite to eat. Laughter at the lack of an enemy raised their spirits.

Osfrid dismounted his steed. "Maybe the buggers ran off." Muttered Acca as he took the reins of Osfrid's horse and led it off to a nearby pond for a drink.

Osfrid strode over to the king adjusting his sword belt as he went. The king's personal bodyguard were ahead of them scanning the streets for any possible dangers and forcing back any citizens that got too close to their king. The throng of people was cheering the army as it made its way through the muddy streets, the Fyrd men smiled whilst the Huscarl's kept the cool composure of professional killers, eyes constantly looking for threats and their hands resting on the hilts of their swords or axes. Finally Harold and the Thegns reached the city centre, the bodyguards forcing a route through the population with threatening language or the butts of their weapons.

Standing outside the rebuilt hall that had once belonged to Tostig stood Morcar and Edwin. The two brothers looked haggard and exhausted, but despite their exhaustion the men held their heads high.

"Those fetchers should be on their knees." Growled Gyrth through gritted teeth. Osfrid nodded in agreement with the king's brother. He looked around and saw Cearl standing to one side, a look of shame on his face.

Harold strode to stand before Morcar, an expression of annoyance and anger on his handsome face.

"Do the Earls of the North no longer bow to their king?" he shouted so that the gathered crowd could hear. "Earls that surrendered my city without a fight. Earls that led their men to defeat at Fulford Gate." As the king rang off the list of indiscretions the lords of the north had made, Morcar's face flushed red in anger.

Harold leaned in close to Morcar and whispered in his ear; "this city is mine, the North is mine. Your dreams of an independent Northumbria die this day, do you hear me?"

Morcar glared at Harold before bowing his head in acquiescence. The two Earls fell to their knees and one by one kissed the Kings ring emblazoned with the royal symbol.

*

"The army will rest a few hours and resupply before we make our next move. The way I see it, we have a number of options on how to proceed." The King had commandeered Morcar's hall and the Thegns of the Saxon army were crammed into the main chamber.

A large oval table made of varnished oak stood at the end of the hall upon which lay a cloth map of the surrounding area. Ealdred the bishop of York and some monks were scribbling down the Kings words and writing up a list of provisions needed if a siege occurred.

Osfrid stood next to Cearl; he was glad to see the man had survived Fulford but noticed a gash on the older man's cheek.

"We could wait here for the Norsemen to attack us', the king continued; 'but that would most likely lead to a long siege.' The Thegns looked at each other in dread, Saxons hated fighting sieges. Harold chuckled as he noticed the alarmed expressions on his men's faces.

"We will be vastly outnumbered and surrounded in days, so I think we can rule that out."

The King talked on with his brother as the other nobles chatted amongst themselves over battle plans and strategies.

Cearl smiled weakly at Osfrid and gripped his wrist in greeting.

"I'm glad to see you yet live Osfrid, messy business at Fulford very messy." He said mournfully.

"Morcar was a fool to engage the Norsemen alone. If he hadn't summoned us so soon I would've been able to....' Osfrid paused as a wave of sorrow threatened to overwhelm him, flashes of his wife's face appeared in his mind's eye, her long red hair billowing in the sunlight, her laughing, of them making love. He was brought out of his thoughts by Cearl.

"My friend what has happened?"

Osfrid explained what had happened to Driffield and his beloved Aerlene. Cearl's face was a mask of sorrow as he relived discovering his own butchered family the year before.

"Now is not the time for my sorrow." Osfrid said composing himself and burying the pain deep inside his soul. "What happened after Fulford?" he added changing the subject. At the front of the room the King and Earls were in animated conversation, Gyrth and Edwin were arguing whilst Harold looked on in tired amusement.

"The day after the battle, Harald and Tostig arrived at the walls of the city. Morcar surrendered without a fight, he offered tribute of food and gold as well as hostages."

Cearl glanced around to ensure no one else was listening to their conversation. 'I reckon Morcar was hoping to join forces with Harald and ensure the safety of his lands. He was hoping that the Norsemen would beat Harold and would then have to slog it out with the Normans when they inevitably invade. Then with both sides weakened he would swoop down and finish them off or maybe he believes that he can negotiate for the North to be spared."

Osfrid looked at his friend in surprise. He knew Morcar was ambitious but surely even he wouldn't be foolish enough to gamble the entire country for his dreams of becoming king of a free Northumbria.

A thought struck him.

"Cearl, when and where were the hostages due to be delivered to the Norsemen?"

Cearl thought for a moment, recalling the negotiations that had occurred the previous days.

"Today, At Stamford Bridge." He answered.

Osfrid smiled. He had a plan. He pushed his way to the front of the hall to stand near to the King.

Gyrth stepped closer to the map and used his dagger to point to a location. Osfrid recognised the lay of the land seeing what the king's brother had in mind.

"Why don't we head overland and strike at the Norse fleet anchored at Ricall."

Harold shook his head.

"We don't have enough ships to prevent them from heading back to sea. We'd march all that way only for them to slip by us and sail further south. No, we need to trap them and destroy them in one battle. The longer we delay dealing with the Norsemen is time William will use to invade the South."

The tired King rubbed his eyes tiredly. The pressure of war was getting to him.

For most of the year he had felt unwell, the stress from preparing for invasion and fighting a war on two fronts was slowly grinding him down.

"Milord, if I may suggest something." Osfrid stepped forward. "We know that a force of Norsemen will be at Stamford Bridge awaiting the transfer of hostages and tribute.' He pointed to the location on the map, 'Our scout's say that the enemy has no idea that you've arrived yet, if we march there with all haste we could take them by surprise. With a bit of luck Hardrada may be there overseeing the transfer in person."

The King regarded Osfrid for a moment before smiling slyly.

"Attack them head on. I like that plan." He said smoothly. He thought for a moment and looked at his brother and commanders. All nodded in agreement.

He turned to face his Earls and Thegns.

"Prepare your men. We march for Stamford Bridge and we will drive those Viking bastards back into the sea!"

34.

September 25th 1066

Stamford Bridge

Hunweld marched next to his son and Acca, his own remaining Varangian's behind him. He glanced at Osfrid, pride filled his heart, the young scared man he had left behind when he fled East had become a strong honourable man, a man who deserved more than what had happened to his family.

'Could I remain so calm if I were in his shoes?' he thought to himself. His thoughts drifted to his wife so far away in Constantinople. He had heard no word from her since he arrived back in England. He made a silent prayer to God to protect her and the boy.

The countryside rolled by, the green fields turning into the beginning of woodland as they approached Stamford Bridge. Hunweld cleared his head and focused on what was to come. The Suns heat diminished slightly as the forest cast its shadow over the sweltering army.

Velmud moved up the column of troops to walk at Hunweld's side.

"I'm sorry lad." Hunweld muttered as he looked at the young Norseman next to him.

"What for sir?" Velmud replied in Angslic, much to Hunweld's surprise. He barked a laugh of surprise.

"When did you learn our language lad?"

Velmud shrugged and smiled, "Working and fighting at the side of Saxons for nearly a year, as well as the tavern girls, you learn things."

The two men laughed causing the nervous looking Acca to turn around. "What's so funny?"

"This little whoreson can speak our language." Hunweld joked, cuffing Velmud round the head.

Acca raised his eyebrows in surprise before falling into step with Velmud. The two men then started chatting and joking.

"Good lads those two." Hunweld said to his son. Osfrid nodded in agreement, but his eyes were clouded as though he were somewhere else entirely.

"Do you think that murderer will be there?" Osfrid spoke quietly. The lust for vengeance shimmered through him.

Hunweld placed a hand on his son's shoulder. "If he is I'll leave him to you, and god help him when you have him in your grip."

Osfrid nodded and gripped his swords hilt tightly, he was ready for battle, and he wanted blood.

*

The Norsemen lay around in the morning sunshine, some slept under the shade of trees, and others sat on the river Derwent's banks eating. A group of them were filling barrels with the rivers water. None wore their armour; today they were going to receive tribute and hostages from the scared locals. Their king was in a jovial mood as he joked with his men.

Harald had taken only a small force with him. No signs of Saxon resistance had been reported and the local population seemed timid and relatively accepting of their situation. The Bridge of Stamford Bridge was a narrow wooden and rickety affair. He glanced at the sky and narrowed his eyes against the glare. The day was peaceful, a good omen for the days of blood that were sure to follow as his great army marched South and deeper into England.

He sat on a makeshift throne under a canvas of cloth taken from one of the ships anchored at Riccall. His son and heir Olaf was back with the ships and the rest of the army, as long as the fleet was safe then his conquest would be assured, the Saxons had shown very little aptitude when it came to naval warfare. With his fleet he would be able to strike anywhere on the islands, the added mobility would be crucial on destroying any resistance in the South.

He leaned back contented calling for a cup of ale to quench his thirst.

The North was his, Morcar and his wimp of a brother had pledged their support to his campaign, the promise of a free Northumbria their aim. He scoffed at their gullibility; little did they know that as soon as he was victorious he would have the snivelling idiots executed and his trusted ally Tostig reinstated as ruler of the North. He would inherit a vast empire, one to match Canute's and the other great Viking kings of old.

He was snapped out of his thoughts by the sound of galloping hoofs. Tostig burst out of the foliage red faced and a look of fear on his face. Immediately Harald rose from his throne.

"Lord King, look to the horizon, what do you see?" Tostig panted.

Harald squinted, there in the distance a huge plume of dust rose from beyond the trees. Had his son sent extra men? His eyes widened in realisation.

"TO ARMS!" he roared, his men looked at him dumbfounded but then they too saw the dust cloud. Panic struck the Norsemen.

"We have no armour... we left it back at the ships." Tostig snarled in frustration angry at their foolishness.

*

The Saxons emerged from the tree line, grim faced and eager for battle.

Osfrid stood at the head of his men on the right flank, the King was in the centre and Gyrth on the Left. To his amazement he saw the Norsemen panicking as they fled across the rickety bridge before them. He noticed few wore armour and only a few had shields.

Harold noticed it too, drawing his sword kicking his heels into his horse's flanks and surging ahead of the army, his mounted Huscarl's beside him. The rest of the army dismounted and formed a battle line. The ten thousand Saxons let out a great cheer as they watched their King and his bodyguard ride down the Norsemen too slow to cross the bridge in time. Sunlight glinted off the blades of the riders; scarlet filled the air where the weapons hacked down the Viking stragglers.

A horn call came from Gyrth's flank. Osfrid saw the cause for the warning. There, on the opposite bank the Viking King had formed a circular shield wall, his standard the Land Ravager flying high at the centre.

Osfrid almost laughed in joy as he spotted the figure of Tostig at the huge Kings side. Vengeance would be his.

Harold and his bodyguard reigned back from their pursuit. Norse archers had formed up in the tree line to the left of the sheildwall daring the horsemen to come into range. '*Stalemate for now*' thought Osfrid as he raised his arm to halt his men. Archers were the scourge of all warriors; the fear of being cut down by an arrow filled the hardiest with dread.

*

Harold rode back to his army and raised his sword to heaven. The Saxons roared for their King. He spun his horse galloping down the line until he reached his brother. He snatched a cloak from one of the earls and wrapped it about himself. He pulled the hood over his head and rode back towards the bridge, his bodyguard surrounding him.

As they approached the bridge he saw a Viking on a black horse fall from his saddle. The man was huge, bigger then a bear!
"Who is that man?" he asked one of his Huscarl's as the Norse King clambered back onto his saddle.

"I think it's the Viking king Harald sire." The bodyguard replied.

Harold laughed, "It seems all luck has deserted him this day!"

The bodyguards laughed. Harold slowed his horse and trotted to the bridge. He cupped his hands and bellowed for a parlay.

The Norse sheildwall opened and out rode a dozen Vikings. At their head was the man on the black horse, Harald Hardrada, he was a big bugger and far more intimidating up close. Harold's heart spun as he saw his brother Tostig riding at the side of his enemy. He gulped down his emotions before trotting up to the foot of the bridge. He wrapped the hood tighter to hide his face. No point giving Hardrada an opportunity to kill him so easily. His bodyguard knew the ruse he was planning, they had seen him do it enough times in the past, like those times he would pretend to be his herald, he hoped Tostig would have enough remaining honour to not expose him too soon.

The two groups faced one another. Hardrada eyed up the hooded man with suspicion. Tostig had a wry smile on his face. Despite his hatred for his brother he could not doubt his bravery.

“I am Fungold, herald of King Harold of the Saxons. I speak for him.” the hooded figure said.

Tostig translated for Hardrada, who nodded in understanding. The hooded man looked at Tostig.

“If you lord Tostig rejoin your brother Saxons you shall be spared. Your lands will be returned to you and one third of England will be yours to rule alongside your brothers. The King gives you this one chance to return to the Godwinson fold.”

Tostig's expression softened. His brother was willing to save him, was a brothers love still there despite all of the things he had done? The offer was tempting, but unrealistic. The Thegns and Earls would demand his death either way. He shook his head sadly.

"What would happen to King Harald and his men?" he asked. He could feel his brothers gaze upon him under the hood.

"We will give him seven feet of ground or as much more as he is taller than most men" came the uncompromising reply.

Tostig smiled sadly. So it would be to the death then.

"I will not sully my name further by bringing the King of Norway to England, only to betray him." With that Tostig spun his horse gesturing to the others and Hardrada to follow. They rode back to the Norse sheildwall.

"That was no Herald." Hardrada stated. 'Who was he?"

"He was my brother Harold." Tostig replied sadly. Hardrada halted his horse.

"If I had known that, I would have killed him right then and there!" the king spat angrily.

*

The horns sounded, Osfrid drew his sword and as one the Saxon army surged towards the bridge. As they ran he noticed the Norse sheildwall opened, a few Viking warriors crossed the bridge.

"They're sending out a vanguard to slow us down!" shouted Acca.

The lightly armoured Norsemen charged screaming at the approaching Saxons. Osfrid's men were following behind Cearl's contingent; the honour of reaching the bridge first was to be theirs. Adrenaline pumped through his body, he took in the situation ahead of him. Cearl's men were only feet away from the bridge when a hail of arrows slammed into the leading men like a fist. A dozen Saxons fell screaming, arrow shafts sticking out of their bodies.

"SHEILDS! "bellowed Osfrid. He raised his round shield just in time; he stumbled as an arrow slammed into the wooden frame, bouncing off harmlessly.

He regained his footing and looked up to see Cearl's men engage the Norse vanguard. Swords and axes clashed, men from both sides fell, and some fell into the flowing Derwent with a scream.

Osfrid reached the bridge, Acca just behind him the younger mans shield protecting his flank from the archers who were shooting their arrows with increasing desperation.

The Saxon warriors behind him had formed a sheildwall to protect themselves from the hail of missiles raining down upon them.

The wall was proving effective; few Saxons were falling to the deadly maelstrom. Saxon archers loosed their own volley, the arrows arching overhead and slamming down into the lightly armoured Norsemen. Javelins were thrown by Huscarl's at the Nordic archers impaling a score on their lethal points. The screams of battle rang out over the previously serene landscape.

The bridge battle had turned into a pushing match between Cearl's men and the Norse vanguard.

Osfrid swore under his breath, the longer they were held on this side of the bridge the likelihood that Viking reinforcements would arrive grew. He looked up as he saw a behemoth of a Viking in full armour and armed with a massive brutal looking war axe cleave his way through Cearl's men. A dozen fell in a single mighty blow, Cearl among them. Osfrid cried out as he saw his friend fall into the river a massive gaping wound splitting him in two.

"It's Thor himself!" muttered Acca in disbelief.

The giant Norseman decapitated two more Saxons and viciously hacked his way through another's torso. Blood and gore covered Osfrid and his men.

Hunweld moved up next to his son. "A bloody Berserker, not seen one like him since before you was born lad." He laughed manically. Osfrid looked at his father as though he were mad.

"Fall back!" screamed the lead Saxons. The berserker cut down another handful of men as he menacingly advanced on the panic stricken front ranks.

"Bugger it all" Osfrid shouted in frustration. The Saxons retreated back across the bridge the berserker laughing mockingly at their backs.

The Saxon army regrouped on the York side of the river and waited, no-one willing to face the Nordic monster. Harold rode to the head of the army and appraised the situation. He wheeled his horse to face his men.

"One man holds you all at bay!" he cried. "One Saxon is worth more than one wretched Norseman, which of you has the courage to kill that bastard!" he shouted pointing at the Berserker who was picking dirt from under his fingernails with a bored expression. The man was covered in blood and gore, his long beard stained red with Saxon blood.

"Why not put an arrow through him sire!" shouted one of the Thegns.

Harold glared at the man. "Shoot him like a coward? Never! We are Saxons, we have honour, he has slain forty of us, will no man prove to those pig fuckers that we are better than they and avenge their comrade's deaths!"

Osfrid frowned in annoyance.

"Sod the Kings sense of honour. The longer that big bastard holds us here the longer the Norsemen have to bring in reinforcements." he muttered.

He turned to face Acca and his father. "We have to get the berserker out of the way." He thought for a moment, noticing some of the barrels the Norsemen had been using to fill with river water lying on the rivers bank. An idea entered his head.

"Acca, father, you see those barrels on the bank?"

Hunweld nodded, "Aye I see them, what do you have in mind?"

Osfrid smiled. "I have a plan."

*

Time was passing, the sun was close to reaching its apex in the sky and still the Viking Berserker held the bridge, three new Saxon corpses lay at his feet, men who had challenged him in single combat, brave but foolish.

The Saxon army's morale faltered with every kill. Acca looked up from his task as another cheer arose from the Norse sheildwall; he winced at the thought of another poor sod being cut in two by the berserker.

"Right lad, get in." Hunweld said as he held the barrel in the water.

The cold waters were up to his waist. They had found the barrels Osfrid had mentioned and emptied one of its contents.

Acca had stripped off his armour until he only wore a tunic and boots. He clambered into the barrel, wincing as he stood on a splinter.

“This is crazy.” He muttered, taking the spear from Hunweld. The older man laughed pushing the barrel into the centre of the river, its current taking the barrel in its grip and sending Acca drifting down stream towards the bridge.

35.

"I accept the challenge." Shouted Osfrid raising his sword into the air, the Saxons stood next to him clapped him on the back in respect.

"Let the honour of the kill be yours Lord Osfrid" Harold said, as he watched from his horse.

Osfrid nodded to Velmud who smiled weakly back.

"Don't worry, this will work, I just have to stay alive long enough for you to signal to Acca. Wish me luck." Velmud gripped Osfrid's wrist in brotherhood before slipping down the river bank to wait for Acca in his barrel.

*

Osfrid walked onto the bridge. His breathing echoed in the confines of his helmet. The face plate was down; only the Berserker filled his vision. His thoughts drifted to Aerlene, her beautiful face drifted through his thoughts like a spectre.

'I may be with you very soon my love.' He whispered. The thought did not fill him with sorrow but with a calm acceptance. She was waiting for him.

He held his sword in front of him and his shield tucked high under his chin. Cautiously he advanced; the Berserker stood with a keen expression on his blood soaked features, the man was eager to kill more Saxons. Osfrid would not give him the chance.

Osfrid roared a challenge darting forwards with a speed that took the Norseman off guard. His dragon sword flashed upwards slicing into the Berserkers unprotected flesh. Blood spurted from the wound but the big man was quick too, throwing his body forwards and forcing the swords blade to skim off his body. Osfrid spun raising his shield and battered the Norseman in the face staggering him.

At once the Berserker regained his footing and gripped the edge of Osfrid's shield wrenching it with all his might. Osfrid bellowed out in pain as the shields straps snapped under the force, crushing his arm.

The berserker barked a laugh as the shield fell free leaving Osfrid exposed on his left flank. The Berserker threw the shield away over the bridge, swinging his mighty axe over his head and bringing it down at Osfrid's head. The Saxon army watched the two skilled warriors in intense silence praying that their man would win the day.

Desperately Osfrid dodged deflecting the axe head with his sword, parrying a series of blows that rained down upon him. Sweat poured into his eyes and his arm ached in pain, he couldn't take much more before the berserker added him to the pile of Saxon dead.

Osfrid countered savagely knocking the axe aside and butting the Norseman in the face with his helmeted head. The berserker roared in pain staggering backwards.

'I need to get him into the centre of the bridge' it was now or never.

Osfrid rained a series of frantic blows with his sword forcing the big man back several steps. He overreached one of his attacks and the Berserker deflected the sword causing Osfrid to stagger forwards and crash to the deck. The berserker brought the hilt of his axe smashing down onto Osfrid's back, his armour the only thing saving him from suffering a broken spine. He collapsed to the floor of the bridge. The Norseman forced his head down onto the surface of the bridge with his foot, axe held high to deliver the killer blow. Osfrid could see the waters of the Derwent flowing slowly by through the cracks in the Bridges wooden planks.

It was then that Osfrid heard the high pitched whistle from the side of the bridge. *'Velmud!'*

Through the gaps he saw a barrel drift into view, he closed his eyes waiting for the axe to fall onto his skull. It never came.

A gargled scream came from above him; he looked up and saw the berserker stood with his axe high in the air, a look of stunned disbelief on his face, blood spurting from his mouth, a spear sticking into his groin from underneath the bridge.

The Berserker gave out a gargled roar of disbelief before collapsing to the bridges deck. The Saxons roared in delight, the Norsemen shouted their disgust.

Osfrid staggered to his feet, raised his sword in victory and charged headlong across the bridge. He picked up a shield from one of his brave dead companions as he ran. The Saxon army right behind him.

The battle of Stamford Bridge had begun.

***

36.

September 25th 1066

Stamford Bridge

Osfrid crouched behind his shield as he crossed the bridge deflecting a javelin hurled by one of the Norse warriors rushing to meet him. At his back roared ten thousand angry Saxons pouring over the bridge, blood lust in their hearts. He peeked over the shields rim and could see that the Norse sheildwall had formed into a wide circle. Their flanks would be protected but the sheer weight of numbers favoured the Saxons.

The two armies crashed together in a deafening crescendo of shouts, crashing wood and metal. Screams quickly followed as the furious hand-to-hand fighting grew more savage.

Osfrid was in the thick of the fighting his sword dented, covered in blood. His armour had been scratched and battered but he didn't care, all he saw was his foes, his blade snuffing out their lives with every brutal thrust. At his back Acca and Hunweld fought just as vengefully. Thoughts of Aerlene and the devastation of Driffield fuelled their rage.

Huscarl battled Berserker, sword clashed with sword, axe against axe, the most skilled and ferocious warriors in the world clashed in mortal combat. Scores fell from both sides but the Saxons were gaining the upper hand. The Norse sheildwall was being to weaken as wave after wave of Saxons charged the line.

Time and again the Vikings held their ground their war axes cutting down their attackers. They knew they were outnumbered fighting ever more desperately as Harold's men fought their way through the Norse lines.

Osfrid roared as he thrust his sword through the throat of a berserker the man's lifeless corpse collapsing at his feet. Without their armour the Norsemen were proving easy pickings. To his left stood Hunweld and Velmud fighting back to back, gods of war both them.

The two Varangian's fought with an unsurpassed skill and majestic brutality. Velmud's axe decapitated a shrieking Norseman; Hunweld's cleaved another almost in two. Blood soaked them all from head to toe. A roar spread through the Saxon Ranks as their king joined them in battle. Harold had shed his cloak and now wore a suit of mail, his sword already stained in an enemy's blood. With their King alongside them the Saxons picked up the pace of their butchery. The Derwent flowed red with blood, the once scenic spot had become a slaughterhouse with no respite in sight.

Acca cried out as the Norse sheildwall was breeched. He threw down his broken long sword and drew the short stabbing bade of the Sax. He dove into the gap thrusting left and right with the smaller blade punching deep into the sides of the two Norsemen on either side of the breach widening the gap further to allow more Saxon warriors to pile in behind him.

Victory was close.

A horn call resonated over the battlefield, with a roar Harald Hardrada the king of the Vikings charged the Saxons desperate to close the sheildwall once more. His standard *Land ravager* stood defiant in the ground with berserkers standing at its base daring anyone to try and topple the flag.

Hardrada raised his axe high in the air in defiance. Again and again the Saxons charged the Norse line but were repulsed each time. Hardrada's skill in warfare encouraged his men to desperate feats of skill and bravery. Even without their armour the Norsemen fought with a determined savagery.

Hardrada opened his mouth to bellow at his men, to encourage them, to rally them to one more push, but words never left the Kings mouth. An arrow shot from a Saxon archer on the other side of the river struck the King in his windpipe. Acca shouted insults at the falling body of the man who had once been a Varangian, a mighty feared warrior, now just a sack of meat crashing to the ground.

The Viking King was dead.

***

37.

Stamford Bridge

Hardrada's corpse lay at the base of *land ravager* its defenders standing stunned at the sight of their dead king. The fighting slowed until an eerie calm descended over the scene of slaughter. The Norsemen stood in confusion, with their king dead they no longer had anyone to command them.

King Harold lowered his sword; "Surrender!" he shouted at his foes. The Norsemen hesitated; some lowered their weapons, whilst others took the opportunity to flee, but most stayed, uncertainty in their eyes.

"There will be no surrender... brother." Tostig stood defiantly next to Land Ravager, his Flemish mercenaries at his back growled in agreement. His red hair was matted with sweat and blood, his armour was dented but still he stood his ground.

As soon as the words sunk in the Norseman screamed their defiance, the battle resumed. Once more screams filled the air and the deafening sounds of clashing metal resonated across the river.

Osfrid stared at Tostig. All thoughts of the battle were now gone his sole purpose for existing now was to impale the man who ordered his wife and daughters kidnapping, his wife's murder onto the end of his sword.

He advanced through the battle field like a man possessed, any Norseman who got in his way he cut down without a seconds thought. At his back were Hunweld and Acca. The two men fought desperately to keep up with him.

Osfrid hacked his way through the Flemish mercenaries, his sword getting stuck in the guts of one of the screaming foreigners. Viciously he yanked the blade out of the mewling man spilling his innards onto the ground. The horror of it all, no longer mattered to him, all he could see before him was Tostig, his wife's face and vengeance.

"Tostig" he roared over the din. Tostig spun to face him his eyes growing wide at the sight of his blood soaked enemy.

"I swear to God that you will pay for your crimes! You murdered my friends, ordered the kidnapping of my family; your man murdered my wife!"

Tostig barked an order at his men to give them room. The mercenaries formed a small shield wall to hold off any interference.

Osfrid barked a humourless laugh.

"You would face me?"

Tostig smiled wickedly. "Look around you Osfrid. Everything you know and love will end! If not today by my hand then it will by the Norman's. My brothers will all die one way or another, this land will burn and our people will be snuffed out like a candles flame."

Osfrid pointed his sword at Tostig.

"You speak of our doom as though we are all cowards. We will fight; we will never be conquered by the likes of you." He growled.

The two men circled one another waiting for a chance to strike.

"Osfrid the unconquerable how amusing.' Tostig scoffed, 'Handel took great pleasure in raping your whore's corpse. I took your wife, your children and yet you still fight on".

"I will not stop until you are in hell!" Osfrid roared. He swung his sword in a vicious cut, Tostig dodged under the swing countering with his own blade forcing Osfrid to take a step back.

The two men were skilled swordsmen and now both unleashed that skill upon the other. The swords clashed and parried. Osfrid's eyes never left his foes. Calmness had descended upon him as he fought. Visions of Aerlene filled his soul with determination. *'You must win for our children'*

He feinted a thrust at Tostig's throat, as his enemy raised his blade to block the strike Osfrid rotated his wrist reversing the move and stabbed his blade deep into Tostig's chest.

Blood sprayed from the wound forcing the red haired man to fall onto the ground in agony. His chainmail had prevented the dented Dragon blade from puncturing deeply. Osfrid stood over his wife's murderer his blade pointed at his throat. Tostig gasped for breath.

"I will never be conquered. Vengeance is mine." Osfrid stared into his foes eyes.

"For Aerlene". He whispered as he thrust his blade down into Tostig's throat.

The blade sunk through bone and gristle, blood poured from his mouth as he drowned on his own bile and the metal slicing through to his spine. He weakly pawed at Osfrid until he stopped moving; he was dead, screaming his way to hell.

An immense weariness overwhelmed Osfrid as he slumped to his knees, his head resting on the hilt of his sword. He stared into the dead eyes of his enemy and sobbed. Emotion consumed him as he watched his wife's killer die. Around him the Flemish mercenaries fled. Most were cut down or drowned in the Derwent's flowing waters.

Victory was there's.

Osfrid lifted off his helmet and took in the carnage around him. Thousands lay dead or dying in the dust and dirt, blood covered the grass, and mangled men were wondering in a daze through the chaos.

The battle had moved deeper into the woods, the sounds of vicious fighting could still be heard. *'No doubt Acca and Hunweld were in the thick of it.'* He thought tiredly.

Slumping back onto his heels he stared up at the bright blue sky, the sun shining hotly onto his exhausted face.

As Osfrid sat on the grass he was unaware of the man sneaking up behind him.

Handel had watched his master's death. He had been at his master's side throughout the early stages of the battle, but upon seeing Osfrid he had skulked to the rear of the lines, waiting for an opportunity. The warrior was alone and now he would die. He drew his knife and prepared to strike.

*

38.

The crunch of grass behind him alerted Osfrid to Handel's presence. He tried to roll out of the way of the incoming blow but his fatigue had made him slow. With a shout Handel brought his blade down stabbing deeply into Osfrid's back. Osfrid roared in pain and felt his legs go numb. He crashed onto his front.

Handel cackled as knelt down in front of his prey. Osfrid gasped for breath, his lung had been punctured by the knife, and his eyes went wide at the sight of the wretch before him.

Handel wore a leather patch over his ruined eye, his bold head and weasel like features gave him a fearsome appearance.

"I killed your wife, not him.' Handel cackled as he pointed to Tostig's corpse. 'I enjoyed doing it too." He held a hand to his missing eye, "Your son owes me an eye, if only I had could have skewered your bastards too then this would be even more fun."

Osfrid was helpless. He could feel his life draining away from the wound in his back. Warm blood filled his tunic and armour. But that didn't matter, Handel had inadvertedly given him hope. His children still lived; Handel hadn't killed them as he had feared. A loud roar emanated from deeper in the woods. Handel glanced behind him before focusing back on his victim.

"Sounds like King Harold has won the day. A pity I would have liked to have been made a lord by the Norsemen. Ah well, there is always William." He sneered. Osfrid coughed up blood.

"The Normans will come, and they will win, and I will work for them."

Osfrid glared at his wife's killer. "I will kill you." He coughed.

Handel's head rocked back in laughter.

"No you piece of shit, I am going to kill you and your brats and your friends." He grabbed Osfrid's hair violently and placed his dagger to his throat.

"Now die."

***

Epilogue

William, Duke of Normandy, stared out across the English Channel, his hands clenched in frustration.

The winds had not been favorable, and after weeks of waiting doubts had crept into his mind that God had abandoned his cause.

The Throne of England was his by right, he would be a King.

Hundreds of ships lay idle in the port towns' docks, thousands of soldiers sat about idling away their time playing cards or drinking ale.

He was stirred from his thoughts by a stirring in the air.

The weather vane atop the church at Saint-Valery squeaked as it's swung about to face Northwards. The Southerly winds he had been praying for had come!

He closed in eyes in a prayer of thanks before bellowing to his vast army to prepare for war.

The Invasion was about to begin, the Normans were coming for the greatest prize in Christendom, the throne of England.

*

About the Author:
Matthew Olney

Matthew lives in Cornwall in the South West of England and lives in the small town of Helston on the Lizard Penisula, with his partner Chloe.

By day he works as a copywriter for a financial company but at night he writes novels.

He graduated from University College Falmouth with a BAHons in Journalism, and has had news stories published in a number of regional newspapers.

History is his favorite subject, and writing the Unconquered series is a life ambition. Osfrid will return in his battle to save his home from the invading Normans.

To contact him you can use;

Facebook @ https://www.facebook.com/Unconqueredseries

or

Twitter @ https://twitter.com/Unconqueredbook

8768253R00195

Printed in Great Britain
by Amazon.co.uk, Ltd.,
Marston Gate.